KISS OF BLARNEY

Penelope Marzec
A Novella

© Copyright Penelope Marzec 2015.
All rights reserved.
Previously published by
New Concepts Publishing 2006
and Crescent Moon Press 2011

Cover Art: Jeannie Ruesch

For my best friend, Emily

Chapter One

Shay could swear someone was watching his every move. A prickly sensation lingered along his shoulders, and he rubbed the back of his neck while standing at the bar in Paddy's Pub in Green Creek, New Jersey--a half a world away from his birthplace in Ireland.

He now called Green Creek home, but he often felt as though his Irish heritage had followed him there. No doubt, the blame lay with his *geise.* His da had insisted that as a descendent of the Irish kings, Shay must be given *geise*--even though he happened to be living in the twenty-first century. All the legendary Irish kings had been given *geise,* a set of rules tailored for the individual, which must be obeyed.

If a man did not conform to the *geise,* it was said that misfortune or even death could result.

Most of the time, Shay considered his situation absurd. Being related to a bunch of illustrious, long gone--as well as bloodthirsty--Irish kings did not put bread on the table. Becoming a mason had been a far more lucrative career for him. Nevertheless, his father had ingrained the *geise* into his mind and Shay could not rid his thoughts of them. Since there was a blizzard outside, and he was in a pub, one commandment in particular came to mind.

Thou shalt not drink strong liquor when snow blankets the sod. Shay wiped the cold sweat from his brow as the echo of his father's warning kept him on edge despite the fact that he opted to drink beer.

However, he decided his unease could also be due to the current situation at the pub. Tonight, stranded parade marchers jammed the largest Irish pub on the Jersey Shore. Green Creek's famous St. Patrick's Day Parade had been cancelled at the last minute due to the major snowstorm. As the white stuff continued to pile up, the marchers bided their time drinking whatever Paddy had to offer while his supply dwindled with each passing moment. The town's electricity had gone off at one in the afternoon and everything had come to a standstill. Shay noted that several of the patrons were completely

3

plastered, and he knew drink could bring out the worst in people.

...misfortune or even death could result.

Taking a small sip from his beer, he narrowed his eyes and glanced around at the tables now illuminated only by candles.

"What are you dreaming about, man?" Shay's buddies, Trevor and Liam, slapped him on the back--none too lightly, but Shay's muscles had been fused into steel by his years as a mason so it did not hurt.

"I'm dreaming of my one hundred twenty chimneys," Shay lied. "Aye. I'd be out there now laying the footings if it wasn't for this rotten weather."

"You've a guaranteed fortune." Trevor brightened. "It's only fair you'll be remembering your old friends with another round of beers--we who knew you when all's you had was a shabby suitcase and a cockamamie story about being a descendent of kings."

Shay glared at his friend and hardened his tone. "You'll not be making fun of my father's tale."

From his stricken look, it appeared Trevor realized he had ruined his chances for a free beer. "It's not everyday we have someone walking into this pub, getting drunk and telling us he's related to royalty."

"I was down on my luck that day and a wee bit homesick as well," Shay admitted. "I'm thinking now you didn't mean to get me drunk that day, but I hadn't had a bite to eat."

Liam shoved a bowl of pretzels right under Shay's nose. "We were only helping out a newcomer to our fair town."

Shay reached for the pretzels. His father had been an honest, hard-working man--and if he liked to tell fairytales he wasn't much different from the rest of the Devlins. They all liked to think there was magic hidden beneath every blade of grass in Ireland. There were those in his clan who even claimed to be descendants of the *Tuatha De Danaan.* Funny thing was, most of the old Irish families believed the same nonsense.

Still, some nights here in New Jersey, so far from Ireland, when the moon was full and the air was soft with mist, even

Shay longed for a bit of that old enchantment. However, there was no mist outside tonight--just snow--tons of it. The nerves bunched up in his shoulders.

"Too much time in the pub and we'll all be seeing leprechauns." Trevor gave a hearty laugh.

"Shay's worked hard these past two years and a hard working man deserves to get drunk now and then. Especially, when he's got his fortune made." Liam grinned.

"You're right." Shay raised his glass toward his friends. "We'll be forgetting the tough times today. Paddy, another round."

Paddy, the owner of the pub, shoved a mug toward him. Shay glared at the green liquid inside. Squinting, he held his drink closer to the pale light coming from the battery lantern on the bar. "And what are you doing giving me this evil-colored potion?"

"That, me boy, is in honor of the day," Paddy announced. "It's green beer."

Shay detected a stony look in Paddy's eyes. However, with the feeble lantern light, the flickering candles and the two beers Shay had already consumed, his eyesight could be suffering from more than simple strain.

"I'll be asking for a hearty pint of Guinness, if you want to be celebrating good St. Patrick."

"In America, green is the color for everything reminding us of the old sod." A note of annoyance came across in the pub owner's words. To be sure, his reserves must be getting low.

"They'll not be knocking back such a putrid looking beverage in Ireland today."

"Then you can be going back there if you're not liking the customs here." Paddy's jowls vibrated with an ominous tremor from his frayed nerves. The storm continued to rage while all the candles on the tables melted into small stubs that would soon burn out. Still, none of the patrons took the opportunity to leave.

"It tastes the same as any cheap lager," Trevor licked his lips after downing a bit of the brew. "Close your eyes and you won't be noticing any difference."

"I've got some green bagels to stave off your hunger before you'll be heading home." Paddy's meaning couldn't be missed. "I'm having a sale on the bagels. Three for a dollar."

"Must be getting stale," Liam muttered low.

Shay shrugged his shoulders. His dog, Bran, would be wanting some company on this bitter evening and a hearty blaze in the fireplace would provide a great deal more warmth than the vile beer in Paddy's Pub. At any rate, he'd be keeping himself out of harm's way.

He turned, intending to bid his buddies goodnight when the door to the pub opened, letting in a blast of wind that blew out some of the candles and sent many of the others wavering. A cry of protest went up from some tartan-clad customers nearest the door when they were left in darkness.

Shay let out a laugh. "Maybe we have a banshee coming to haunt us for drinking such a foul brew."

Clad in a long cloak, a petite figure moved toward the bar. The face of the stranger lay in shadow under a capacious hood, and at her side she carried a large, old-fashioned tapestry bag. Upon nearing the bar, her pale hand reached up and swept off the hood, unleashing a mass of rich red, curly hair that glinted in the candlelight. Dazzled by the sight, Shay blinked.

"I don't think she's a banshee," Liam whispered with a note of awe in his voice.

Shay cleared his throat. "Probably just another stranded parade marcher."

"Parade? I'll not be marching in a parade, sir." Her voice had a lilt to it, and while Shay couldn't quite place the unusual accent, it did intrigue him. On such a bitter night, he felt more homesick than usual, and he wouldn't mind talking with someone about the lovely isle he'd left behind.

He found he could not take his eyes off the lady, and he wasn't the only man in the pub staring at the newcomer. With her ethereal eyes, and creamy skin she drew the attention of every man in the room, but she directed her gaze at him as she stated in a near whisper, "I am terribly hungry and thirsty."

A bizarre sensation gripped Shay, an almost overwhelming and primitive lust fired through him. Taking a deep breath, he fought it off. "There's not much left here. Except for green beer and green bagels."

The woman frowned, marring her smooth brow with tiny furrows. She stepped closer to him, swirling her heavy cloak with the movement. He caught a whiff of violets. Though she peered at his face, she did not say a word. An alarming shock went through him, for it felt as if he had touched a power outlet with one hundred-ten volts. He gulped, thinking there must be a logical explanation for it. *Sure, and it could be a bit of static.* His heart lurched. *Or I've had too much beer.* He rocked back and took in a breath to steady himself as a chill ran along his shoulder.

Her lower lip quivered while a look of astonishment crossed her face. Whirling around, she turned to the bagpiper who stood at her other side. Her beautiful eyes narrowed as she looked up into the bagpiper's face to examine his features. She had the longest lashes Shay had seen on a woman. In fact, everything about her seemed unusual, so unique that nobody else in the world could match her in any way. He found his reaction to her very peculiar--never before had he experienced such an immediate hunger for any other woman.

"I'll be asking you for a glass of that same beverage you're drinking." Her lips stretched into a wide grin as she spoke to the bagpiper, but her grip on the tapestry bag tightened.

"It will be my pleasure." The bagpiper motioned to Paddy. "Another glass of this festive brew for the lovely young lady here."

Shay's hand shook as he reached for his own beer and knocked back the vile brew. It did not help to steady his nerves.

Paddy scowled at the presumptuous woman. "I'll be needing proof."

The young woman stammered. "And … and what proof is that?"

"Same as anyone else. You see the sign right there..." Paddy pointed to the notice above the bar. "I'll not be risking my liquor license. I'm carding you, lass."

"Carding?" The woman read the poster. "Proof of age?" A blank expression came over her features.

"Your ID, your license." Paddy crossed his arms over his chest.

Shay cast a sidelong glance at her. She appeared young with her delicate features and small stature. However, her curious, outmoded costume lent her a semblance of maturity. Besides, few young people would be caught dead wearing such an elaborate outfit. Her long, woolen cloak covered a green velvet dress with a wide skirt that reached to the floor. It looked like something out of a fairytale book--or something from the Dark Ages.

"Why you can see I'm fully grown." The young woman tilted her chin upward with pride.

Liam and Trevor hooted with laughter. However, Shay clenched his teeth when he noticed the lecherous sneer on the bagpiper's face.

Then a very odd thing happened. The young woman's brow furrowed as she gave Paddy a fierce glare. He reached for a glass and began to fill it.

"There you go, miss." The old bartender handed her the beer. When he poured her a shot of Jameson's whiskey as well, Shay could only stare in complete amazement.

"Thank you, sir." She downed the whiskey first in one gulp. "My! What a wonderful concoction that is. I feel warm all the way to my toes."

"Then have another for your fingers." Paddy poured her one more shot.

Shay's mouth dropped open. *Had Paddy gone mad?*

The woman tossed down the second shot and proceeded to swallow half of her beer. She came up for air and sighed. "I was so thirsty." She turned again to the bagpiper and smiled. "I'll be needing something substantial to accompany the drinks, sir. Some bread, a bit of cheese...."

"If I'll be buying you dinner, I'll be expecting more than a smile." The bagpiper grabbed her about the waist and drew her up to him to plant a slobbery kiss on her lips.

The young woman cried out and gave him a resounding

slap on his cheek. The entire pub grew silent.

"Why you..." The bagpiper glowered at her as he rubbed his swollen jaw.

Shay stiffened, ready to block the bagpiper's rage and protect the foolish young woman.

"You'll not be taking liberties with me, sir." She smoothed down her dress and straightened out the clasp at the neck of her cloak. Then, lifting her chin, she stared right back at the bagpiper, her eyes like two lasers aiming for the kill.

Confusion broke out on the bagpiper's face. "Paddy, I'll be ordering up a sandwich."

"Green bagels and cream cheese is all that's left, and if you're not liking it, you can go elsewhere." Paddy leaned over the bar in an intimidating manner, but it didn't seem to impress the bagpiper, who had a peculiar blank expression on his face.

"I've never had a green bagel, but I'm sure it would suit me just fine." The young woman's eyes lit up.

A low murmur broke out in the pub as the strange drama played out. Paddy handed over a green bagel, the bagpiper paid for it, and the young woman settled down on a barstool to enjoy her food and beverage.

Shay forced himself to tear his gaze away. Apparently, nobody could resist the lady's charm. He was having a tough time of it himself, but he had no intention of throwing his cash away on some wacky female--no matter how gorgeous she was--though he had to admit she really stirred up his libido. He turned back toward his buddies.

"You'll not be leaving yet." Liam winked. "We're ordering up another round. Your dog'll be fine until you get back."

"A dog?" The high notes of the young woman's voice carried above the general din of the pub.

"A very fine dog." Trevor nodded. "Bran."

"Finn's hound?" A touch of awe sounded in the woman's voice as she focused her gaze at Trevor. Shay shot a furious look at his friend. The man should be keeping his mouth shut.

"Bran is a fine Irish wolfhound." Trevor had a vacant expression on his face. "A pedigree."

Shay studied the woman, wondering if it was her beauty that hypnotized everyone. Her eyes, paler than the blue of a robin's egg, reminded him of shadowed ice. Apprehension knotted up in his shoulders.

"I've a need for a dog--to help me with some hunting." She slid off the barstool and planted herself firmly in front of Shay.

"Hunting is it?" Shay crossed his arms, but he avoided her gaze by studying the clasp at her neck--a golden wheel. The sight of it unnerved him. The Irish Celts used the symbol as a protective talisman against the forces of darkness. Where had she gotten it? It looked like a museum piece. He grew more suspicious of her by the moment. "I'll not be loaning my dog out for a hunting expedition. At any rate, he hasn't been trained for it."

"Please, sir." Her hand rested on his arm, and warmth shot to his heart. She whispered low, "It's a matter of life or death."

Rattled by her touch and her plea, Shay tried to put her off. "Then you should be asking the police for help." She was more than a wee bit touched in the head. Surely, one didn't borrow a dog when life hung in the balance.

A hush had come over the pub as the other patrons strained to listen to the woman's words. She stepped even closer to Shay. Too close, for his head reeled from the haunting scent of violets hovering about her and her breasts pressed against his chest until the room suddenly had all the steam of the tropics.

"'Tis not a matter for the police," she murmured.

He made the mistake of looking into her eyes and found himself so befuddled that all he wanted to do was hold her in his arms. He gripped the edge of the bar instead.

"I bought the young lady the beer and the bagel. She's mine for the night." The bagpiper's growl barely registered in Shay's brain for he could only see the vision of loveliness before him.

The woman whirled to face the bagpiper and Shay came back to his senses, feeling as if someone had siphoned out his wits.

"I do not *belong* to you, sir." Her stern expression had the bagpiper backing off. However, one of his fellow bagpipers chose to support his right of ownership.

"If a man buys a woman a meal, he deserves some of her time." By the leer on his face, there could be no doubt about his true meaning.

* * * *

Having read about the world and the people in it, Ula believed her entrance into society would be a relatively easy matter as long as she kept her origins a secret. Meara had warned her that blathering could get her into trouble, a straitjacket, or worse. Despite keeping mum, Ula realized she now found herself in a dicey situation.

A princess uses her power only when there is no other recourse left to her.

She bit her lip. Perhaps that was at the root of the problem. She had believed the situation warranted the use of the special talent granted her at birth, but maybe she should not have taken the chance. Especially since she felt a bit lightheaded from drinking that strange brew which made focusing more and more difficult. Her power had not worked at all on the dog owner, a fact that worried her since it was the only weapon she could wield against Balor. Her mouth turned as dry as a dead leaf at the thought of meeting up with that evil fiend.

She reminded herself that the bagpiper was only a common man. Drawing herself up, she narrowed her eyes and attempted to force her will upon the second bagpiper. However, within a moment the thoughts she had cast on the original bagpiper wore off, and he lunged for her.

She whirled around in an effort to escape him and tripped on the hem of her long dress. Crashing against a table, she knocked it over and landed painfully on the floor. Thrown off by her maneuver, the bagpiper stumbled into the dog owner and his friends. The air in the pub crackled with tension.

Struggling to untangle her voluminous skirt and get up off the floor, she found the handsome dog owner giving her his hand to help her back to her feet. When their fingers met, a strange sensation shimmered up her arm. Though his rough, callused palm scratched against her tender skin, his clasp was gentle and warm. The intensity of the contact disturbed her, sending a ripple of excitement through her until her senses spun.

As the first man she had spoken to--or met for that matter, he was far more handsome than any of the photographs of males she had seen in her treasured catalogs, but unfortunately his eyes were blue, a fact that fell like a lead weight on her heart.

At least, he had some manners while the great boor of a bagpiper did not.

The dog owner's friends righted the table.

"You moved in after I had already put down my money for that girl," snorted the bagpiper. "I intend to be enjoying her company for the rest of the evening."

Ula stood up and the dog owner released her hand. Bereft without his touch, she poured her longing into a brief glance, but he apparently continued to be immune to her commands. The breath hitched up in her throat as doubts swirled in her mind.

"You fed her, that doesn't give you a license to maul her," the dog owner said.

"Do you want to make something of it?" The bagpiper raised his fists.

A shiver of fear tingled along her spine and Ula gulped. She had read about boxing. People could be knocked out cold in the vicious sport. The dog owner would be hurt. Rushing to stand between the two men, she made another attempt to catch the bagpiper's attention so she could change his mind, but the barkeeper barked out an order and shattered her concentration.

"You men will be leaving my pub! Get out of here before I call the cops."

Ula directed a stern look toward the bagpiper's eyes, but he glared at the dog owner with fury puffing up his face. What if he pounded the dog owner senseless? She would never get a dog and never find Meara! Balor would kill the woman who had kept her safe for so long--and then he would go after the real prize. Ula knew exactly what Balor wanted.

Numb with fear, she clutched Meara's bag against her chest. Her throat ached as she held back a sob. No--she would not give up hope.

"Stop it!" She shoved one hand against the bagpiper's chest, hoping that he would at least glance at her. However, he flicked her away like a pesky fly. She stumbled backward into the same table she had fallen against the first time. It tipped over once more, and she crumpled to the floor with a groan. She had not realized how strong a man could be. *What kind of blessing was her talent? Strength was a far better gift.*

The room seemed to be tilting at an awkward angle. When the dog owner helped her up again, she clung to his hand, hoping that the pub would quit whirling around. He plopped her into a chair in a careless manner. She put her hands to her head. What was wrong with her? Her mind seemed to be all soft and airy, as if it had been stuffed with a bunch of snowflakes.

Angry words escalated into shouts from the bagpiper, the dog owner, and their friends. The punches started flying as a melee broke out right in front of Ula, and she didn't know what to do about it. She couldn't seem to focus on anyone's face but it didn't matter because nobody happened to be paying any attention to her anyway. They went at each other like angry bucks clashing antlers in the bog.

And what doe are the bucks fighting over? Me? Her stomach rolled. Though she had read much about civilization, she had never realized it would be this dangerous.

Inevitably, one of the bucks would win, and she would be claimed as the prize. That must not happen! She had to fulfill her destiny. Most importantly, she had to save Meara from Balor or all would be lost.

Forcing herself to shake off the lethargy that had wrapped itself around her, she pressed her lips together. Gingerly, she stood up and tried to get her bearings. Above the ruckus, a new piercing sound like loud whistles hurt her ears. Without any further warning, she was grabbed from behind and tossed over someone's shoulder.

Chapter Two

"Move it!" voices yelled. "Get out now!"

The biting cold of the wind-whipped snow hit Ula's skin as she was jostled along. Whoever had picked her up was running, and between being bounced unmercifully on a man's shoulder and the intoxicating drink's effects, she felt like retching. Worse, she had lost her grip on Meara's bag and did not know where it was.

When she finally didn't think she could take it any longer, she found herself dumped in a snow bank. The dog owner collapsed down beside her. Meara's tapestry bag landed in her lap. She gave a cry of joy and hugged it to her chest. Closing her eyes, she pictured Meara's kindly face wreathed in a smile. Oh, how she wanted to see her dear druidess again!

She opened her eyes and glanced up to see one of the dog owner's friends holding a small light in his hands. Ula recognized the object as a flashlight. She had seen a photograph of such a wonder in one of her catalogs.

Surely, it was a miraculous invention, glowing as it did in the night. Ula could not help wanting it for her own. The faint echo of Meara's words whispered in the back of her mind. *A princess is never greedy.* But the effect of the strong drinks made Meara's words fade until Ula could barely hear them.

Though her head felt far heavier than usual, she stared up at the man's face and managed to focus on him. "I'm wishing I had that flashlight on this gloomy night."

In less than a heartbeat, the man handed the amazing device to her. It comforted her to know that her lone power continued to work--at least on most people--when she could wrest their attention away from their violent urges. She caressed the flashlight with her nearly frozen fingers, and discovered to her sorrow that it gave off no heat. Still she swung it about and noticed how the beam illuminated everything in its path. With it, she could continue searching for Meara long into the night. However, despite all the excitement, a yawn escaped her. All she wanted to do was lay her head down and go to sleep.

"Stay here until your tracks are covered before you head back--which shouldn't take long at the rate this snow is falling," one of the men warned. "You don't want to be sitting in jail instead of building those chimneys!" The dog owner's friends left.

Ula was left alone with the man on the snow bank. Dizzy and exhausted, she made an attempt to straighten out her cloak and her beautiful velvet dress. It would be ruined after this. She mourned all the hours she had spent sewing the luxurious fabric and a pain stabbed at her heart as she thought once more of Meara. Would she be able to save the druidess? Would her power work against Balor? Or would he capture her as well? Ice settled in her heart at that thought.

"Who would have known that one woman could cause so much trouble?" her companion grumbled.

Shock coursed through her at his accusation. She found her temper flaring as the potent liquor loosened her tongue. "Indeed sir, I was not the one *grinding* my fist into someone else's face as if that pub were a boxing ring." She discovered she had a difficult time getting her mouth to form the words.

"Why did you ask him to buy you a drink in the first place? You could see the vile temper the man has--not to mention his companions--every one of them as mean as a wild pig."

"Are you're thinking you're such a gentleman? 'Twas you who *shoved* me into a chair!" Even in the darkness, she found his virility affecting her. Her heart beat a wild staccato with him so close.

"You didn't seem to be able to stand up!" he shouted back at her. "I'm thinking you are drunk."

Ula gasped. "I've never been drunk!" Despite the fuzziness in her head, Meara's words sounded clearly in her mind. *Princesses do not get drunk.*

"Have you ever had whiskey and beer before?"

"There's countless times I've had root beer."

The man swore.

Ula's mouth gaped open. She had read such words in a book, but she had never heard them spoken until now. "You'll not be using language like that in my presence."

"You started a massacre!" The rough edge of his voice made her heart heavy. "I'm thinking you're nothing but a red-haired devil."

She closed her eyes. Meara's life and Ula's own future hung in the balance. Pressing her lips firmly together, she held back tears. She was no devil but she had dared to use her power on the bagpiper and the bartender. Though she feared she would not have enough money to last through the spring without Meara, she should have paid for the food. It would have been less conspicuous.

Could she survive on her own? She had been taught to be nearly self-sufficient, but it was the idea of living without any companionship that undid her. Of course, if Balor captured her, she would have his company.

Forcing back her panic, she vowed to find and free Meara--with or without a dog. If Balor had Meara in his grip, she merely had to stare at the brute and command him to return the older woman. Willing herself to swallow her dread, Ula opened her eyes and realized she had become hopelessly disoriented. The thick snowfall covered everything in the woods surrounding her as well as the man beside her.

She struggled to get up from the snow bank, but her legs felt heavy, as if they had been weighted down with boulders. She did not like this odd wooziness that made her limbs nearly useless.

The man got up as well and offered her his hand. His touch felt like a caress and gave her comfort. "Aside from the fact that you are plastered, you can forget about driving tonight even if you have four wheel drive."

She looked up at him and found it almost impossible to wrench her gaze away. In the soft glow of her flashlight, she saw the snowflakes dotting his curly hair and laying upon his wide shoulders like downy epaulets. Surely, he was far more handsome than any of the men in her JC Penney catalog.

"I-I have two legs, sir," she blurted out after a moment.

"Yes, and they're wobbly." He didn't sound as harsh. In fact, she rather liked the inflection in his voice. His deep blue eyes reminded her of the beautiful wild lobelia. She sighed, aware that he would play no part in the destiny she must fulfill. According to Meara, Ula would marry a man with black eyes. Recalling the bagpiper, she shuddered. He had black eyes, but he was a dreadful man.

And Balor had black eyes, too. Putting a hand to her throat, she vowed in silence, *I will not let him take me!*

She tried a few steps. Indeed, her knees had as much strength as boiled dandelion greens. *It must be that I am drunk,* she admitted to herself. What a foolish thing she had done!

"It's not a good night for walking--especially if you're tipsy and can't walk in a straight line," the dog owner advised.

Ula struggled to concentrate, but with the handsome stranger at her side it seemed hopeless. She breathed in the scent of him, a musky aroma that intrigued her. The man's nearness sent her pulse racing. Men were so... different! Meara had never told her much about the strange species.

Concentrating, she moved to set one foot down in the snow and then with equal deliberation, she strained to put the other one directly in front of it. The task seemed impossible. As she staggered to the side, the man caught her around her waist before she fell.

She enjoyed his firm touch and the heat of his breath against her cheek. With his support, she felt nearly weightless. A nagging warning sounded from the back of her mind. *Time is of the essence!*

Knitting her brow together, she struggled to shake off her stupor. "I'm sure I can do it right if I practice, sir."

"Why don't you just call me Shay?"

The sound of his name pleased her. She tried it out on her tongue. "Shhhaaay. Oh 'tis a soft name. Softer than snow. My name is Ula." The warmth of his arm radiated through her heavy cloak and started a strange heat in her lower regions that disturbed her. Still, she leaned into him, reveling in the glow permeating through her from the contact.

"You're going to the hotel, Ula. You can sleep there tonight," he said.

"I've never been to a hotel." Naturally, she had read about

hotels and knew of all the amenities available for guests--
things like room service. Oh, how she would love to try room
service, but right now she must find Meara.

"I should be getting home." She looked straight into his
eyes. *With your dog!*

He paid no attention to her command. That unsettled her,
even in her hazy state.

"The governor has declared a snow emergency. You aren't
going anywhere tonight."

"That's ridiculous. I can go home anytime I please." But
Shay's dog would be an invaluable help. Why didn't her power
work on him? She took another step and her feet slid out from
under her. Shay caught her before she landed on her bottom.

"Right." Shay set her back on her unstable legs.

Frustrated and exhausted, she admitted to herself that she
was quite incapacitated. She must not drink such strong liquor
again. As she clung to the man at her side, a strange
thrumming built inside her. Was that the effect of the liquor,
too?

"If I were you, I would lay off the sauce." His warm
breath tickled her ear and set off a delightful trembling along
her limbs.

"Oh, I love sauce." She thought of hot summer days and
Meara's little garden. Once more, the sad ache hit her and she
fought not to cry. "Strawberry sauce, especially." *Princesses
never eat too much. Princesses must never gain too much
weight.* Meara's admonitions replayed in her mind. What if she
never heard them again from Meara's own lips?

"You are so smashed," he said.

She heard the note of exasperation in his tone, but it didn't
matter to her. Conscious of his arms encompassing her and
guiding her along, she reveled in his strength. Her body tingled
with awareness as the muscles in his arms contracted.
Obviously, changing minds had its limits, but the power in a
man's burly sinews could be far more useful. Being so close to
him had the blood surging in her veins, warming her to her
very core, causing her to nearly forget about the blizzard
raging around her.

"What a wonderful thing it must be to be strong," she declared.

"I'm thinking it's far better to be sober." With that, he hoisted her up into his arms.

Ula gasped. He lifted her as if she weighed no more than a thistledown. A strange rippling coursed through her as she was gathered against his chest. With one hand grasping Meara's bag, she wound her other arm around Shay's neck, finding herself hungry to touch more of him, to feel more of him. She toyed with the hair curling above his collar.

Another of Meara's warnings sounded in her mind. *A princess does not flirt with men.* She moved her hand away from Shay's hair. Was she flirting? Meara had not delineated what that sort of behavior entailed. Still, a touch of guilt had her protesting weakly. "I'll not have you taking any liberties with me, sir!"

"The name's Shay. Remember? And I'm only taking the liberty of getting you off my hands." He snarled at her.

Startled by his surly behavior, she felt a deep stab of despair in her heart.

A princess always remembers to say 'please,' 'thank you,' and 'you're welcome.' Undoubtedly, she had forgotten some of her manners. Perhaps she had been a wee bit reckless.

Ula grew silent as her eyes welled once again with tears. She'd been a very bad princess on this, her first foray into the world. To be sure, it had been a necessary trip--although she still had not acquired the dog that would aid her in her search. She glanced up into Shay's face. The muscles in his jaw clenched as he lugged her through the storm. She must get him to loan her his dog... somehow.

They came to a large building that Shay told her was the hotel. Entering the dim lobby, lit only with soft candlelight, he plopped her down in a chair. The temperature of the air in the hotel was not much better than that of the air outside. Shivering, she glanced at the people scattered about the lobby. They slept in chairs, on the floor, and on the staircase. Some had blankets and some did not. Ula thought of her small bed back in the little *bothy*. It would be far more comfortable than a hard floor. She wanted to lay her head on her soft goose feather pillow. Should she go home? Was there a chance she would ever find Meara without the dog?

How long would it be before Balor came searching for her?

Trying to shove that horrible thought to the back of her mind, she decided the world had too many people in it all crowded together. Perhaps that was why they punched each other with so little provocation.

Shay came back to her, scooped her back into his arms and grumbled something about there being no vacancies.

"We'll try the other hotel in town."

Ula didn't care. Her long hike in the snow that day had been far more difficult than she'd expected. Her feet hurt, her head hurt, and her damp clothing left her chilled to the bone. She truly did not think she could hold her eyes open much longer. Drowsy, she found contentment in Shay's arms.

Upon entering the second hotel, they found conditions there as bad as the first one.

"They've no room, either," Shay explained. "What am I going to do with you? Is there someone I can call?"

Ula thought of Meara and her eyes welled with tears. Balor would certainly torture Meara. Right now, Meara could be suffering and in terrible pain.

"No. There's no one to call." She could not force her voice to go above a whisper.

Shay's exasperation showed in the grim line of his lips.

"I just want to sit for a wee bit and maybe... close my eyes for a minute." She could not take another step. Her feet were numb.

"I don't want to be leaving you alone. I'm thinking it wouldn't be a wise idea, especially in your present condition-- and with that bagpiper and his friends lurking around town."

Ula did not argue with him. Safe in his arms, she had started to dream of her little *bothy*. She could see herself in her chair by the hearth warming her frozen feet, and watching a pot of Meara's venison stew simmering. Surprisingly, Meara was there, too--giving a stir to the pot, putting a batch of biscuits into the oven, and then sitting beside her to work on the stitches for her grand velvet dress.

A princess is always neat and tidy. A princess does her chores without complaint. Ula repeated the phrases after Meara. She could recite all of Meara's instructions by heart. *A princess never fails to make her bed in the morning. A princess stands up straight; always remember your royal bearing. A princess walks with dignity. A princess always remembers her manners.*

Ula no longer saw the whirling snowflakes. She saw the green of summer as she rowed along the lazy river in the small dinghy, catching fish with worms she had dug from Meara's garden, but when Ula pulled on her line a dragon jumped out of the water, opened his mouth and tried to swallow her. He looked like the bagpiper, with eyes as black as the devil. She slapped him and his silvery scales rained down upon her.

Ula tried to scream, but she could not get her mouth to open. Fear had her heart racing as she stared at the teeth of the dragon. She could not run away either, something held her back--her feet seemed leaden. She felt a hand on her back as someone patted her and offered soothing words. The dragon receded into the dark waters. Surely it was Meara who tucked her back under the covers as she drifted off into quiet slumber.

* * * *

Shay paced the floor of his living room, running a hand through his hair. *Thou shalt not drink strong liquor when snow blankets the sod.* He had beer in the pub, not whiskey. He did not break that *geise.* He felt fairly safe on that score.

However, anxiety coursed through him as he remembered another *geise. Thou shalt not bring a woman into your house unless you have said your vows to her.* His father had pointed that particular commandment out more frequently as Shay had grown into manhood.

Tonight he had ignored that mandate. He stopped his restless motion for a moment and stared at Ula, now sleeping peacefully on his couch.

...misfortune or even death could result.

He ground his teeth together and began walking back and forth again. He could accept that altogether the *geise* encompassed sensible rules for living, but if he broke one or even two of them what difference would it make. Who would know?

That odd sense of being watched had him turning his head to stare out his windows into the darkness.

Nevertheless, on a night like tonight he did not think he had a choice. Fear knotted in his stomach as he recalled the evening's events. He could not leave the inebriated Ula on a chair in a hotel with a bunch of lecherous bagpipers roaming the town. Sometimes good rules had to be broken, he decided, depending upon the circumstances. He took a deep breath and allowed the weariness to settle down upon him.

He had a blazing fire going in the hearth, which had taken the chill out of the house despite the lack of power. He went to a window and watched the snow pile up. He had listened to the radio in the truck and knew that the storm would continue into the morning.

Then he heard Ula muttering a long litany of rules for princesses and shook his head. *She was not only drunk, she was daft.*

He glanced at her on the couch and felt a twinge of pity as he watched her sleeping. Had the strong drinks addled her brain? He moved to the couch and decided that her breathing seemed more regular now than it had been a half hour ago. He stared at her bosom; it rose and fell in a hypnotic cadence that mesmerized him.

He found himself consumed with a desire to touch her breasts. He had already taken off her boots and socks and found her feet to be exquisite. Surely, more perfection lay beneath the soft velvet bodice.

His hand reached out to touch the soft skin peeking above the smooth fabric. He wanted to know the warmth of the tempting valley that lay between the two faultless mounds, but a wave of guilt washed over him and he drew back. *What kind of fool am I?* Bringing home a drunken woman he did not know was bad enough. But breaking one of his *geise* to do it made him anxious. A creeping feeling of dread swept over him and he knew he would not get any sleep tonight worrying about it. Why had his father given him *geise?* It made no sense in the modern world.

Clasping both hands together behind his back, he turned to stare at the cheery blaze in the fireplace. He would get her out of his house, but he needed to wait until tomorrow when the roads were cleared.

The flames dancing before his eyes brought to mind the color of Ula's hair. He heard a slight rustling movement and could not resist another glance at her.

Curled on her side with her magnificent hair cascading like a molten lava flow about her, she snuggled further down into the quilt he had tucked around her. He leaned over and lifted some of the bright strands of her hair in his hand. It felt like silk. The way it drew his gaze made it seem magnetic.

A sudden idea came to his mind. What if he whispered vows to her? It would not have any legal significance, but perhaps it would satisfy the rules of his *geise.* The wording for *geise* tended to be deliberately vague. Each *geise* could lend itself to different interpretations.

Thou shalt not bring a woman into your house unless you have said your vows to her.

His brow furrowed. It did not state that he must be married. He thought back to all the weddings he had attended. Rubbing his neck, he closed his eyes and tried to remember all the words. What did the groom say?

He opened his eyes and cleared his throat. "I promise to be your husband, in good times and bad, in sickness and in health, for richer or for poorer, till death do us part." It went something like that. He was sure of it.

Ula stirred in her sleep. Her movement startled him. He dropped the lock of hair, and it tumbled back into the mass of waves. Not wishing to wake her, he padded away in his bare feet to his room in the back of the bungalow. He opened the bedroom door and found Bran, his crazy gray wolfhound, waiting for him.

"Shhh," he whispered. "You'll not be disturbing her

sleep." He knew he should not have brought her into his house, but with the blizzard still raging there did not seem much else he could do after she had fallen sound asleep in his truck.

He could only hope that by saying the vows he would avoid any misfortune. He had finally gotten a guaranteed steady paycheck and he did not want to lose it, but to be sure, he was superstitious about breaking one of his *geise.*

He took one last, longing look at Ula. With the blaze in the fireplace, she would be warm and comfortable. He could only pray that she wouldn't be ungrateful for his hospitality in the morning when her head cleared.

* * * *

Ula dreamed of the handsome Shay standing at the altar of the church. However, he had his back to her as she walked up the aisle to marry him. She could see, even from behind, he wore a superbly tailored tuxedo she had seen in the JC Penney catalog. She clutched a bouquet of violets and every flower quivered from the trembling of her own hands. Shay began to state his vows though she had not yet reached the altar. She hiked up her skirts and ran towards him, but as she did so the walls of the church dissolved, and she found herself racing into a clearing in the snow-filled Pine Barrens. When she finally reached her bridegroom, he had finished his vows. She reached up to touch his shoulder, and he turned around.

She saw not Shay, but Balor glaring at her with his hard black eyes. Too terrified to scream she opened her eyes. With her heart thundering, she sat.

Already shaking from fright, she glanced around and realized she had no idea where she was. She ran her trembling hand along the edge of the fine couch, so similar to a piece of furniture she had seen in a catalog. Her cloak had been removed and used to cover her like a blanket. A quilt had been thrown on top of her as well and a pillow had been placed beneath her head. Beside her on the floor, sat Meara's bag. She reached for it and brought it close to her bosom.

Wiggling her toes, she realized someone had taken off her boots and wet stockings. Prickles of fear raced along her spine as she stared around the room. She remembered being carried in Shay's arms. He'd placed her in his truck. She knew she had been so tired that she must have closed her eyes. Was this where Shay lived?

Meara would be horrified if she knew that Ula had spent the night here. Then the horrible truth came rushing at her. She might never see Meara again! Ula's eyes misted as she thought of the dear woman, but then she swallowed the lump in her throat. *Princesses do not cry.* Wiping away the moisture from her eyes, she reminded herself that she was an Irish princess with a lineage that went back to the very hill of Tara where the Irish had been cursed for all time, never to rule their own land.

She took in an unsteady breath while her head pounded and her stomach churned. Vowing never again to drink strong liquor, she knew she had only wanted to try what everyone else was drinking—just once—and that was bad enough. Now she found herself in an even worse situation—waking up in a man's house, having accomplished nothing in her attempt to save Meara.

No matter how awful she felt, she must continue on her mission.

Casting her glance around, she noted the room lay as neat as a pin, though everything had a stark look, devoid as it was of any soft touches—like the doilies she and Meara had crocheted and placed in every conceivable corner of the *bothy*.

To the side, she saw a large black screen. A quiver of excitement coursed through her. That had to be a television! She wondered how it worked. She would very much love to see pictures on it.

As she tossed aside the quilt and her cloak, a chill shook her shoulders. Only a few glowing coals remained in the fireplace. Getting up carefully, she tested her limbs to see if they had returned to their former sturdiness. Assured she could walk as usual, she went to put another log on the dying embers. Her boots had been placed near the fire and her stockings hung over the mantelpiece. She fingered the soft wool and found it nearly dry.

As she thought how considerate Shay had been toward her, something fluttered inside her near her heart. She doubted the feeling came from the strong brew she had consumed last night because this sensation brought a longing with it that she had never experienced until now. She would enjoy being held again by Shay.

Sighing, she marveled at the huge windows flanking the fireplace in the room. Outside, the snow appeared to be tapering off, though the new day's sky remained gray and depressing. Ula walked up to one window and pressed her hand against the glass. The window had to be a full three feet wide. Her little *bothy* had but a few tiny windows.

Staring at the snow in bleak desolation, she realized it must have piled up a great deal more during the night. Searching for Meara would be difficult if not nearly impossible under the current conditions.

She needed more than a miracle. Feeling hopeless and alone, she found her throat aching with despair. She struggled against the anguish, but a sudden racket startled her until she thought the very demons of hell had come to steal her away.

The booming sound of deep drums pounded out a heavy beat and the loud scream of someone howling as if they were in pain chilled her to the bone. Terror held her motionless. Never in her life had she known such an awful din. The very walls of the house shook with the noise.

Then the unearthly clamor stopped. The bark of a dog followed it.

"Go away, Bran. I'll be sleeping for ten more minutes." Shay's weary voice filtered through a closed door to Ula's left.

Ula's heart lifted. Bran! The dog! Her miracle—maybe.

Edging toward the closed door on tiptoe, she put her ear to it and heard deep rhythmic breathing. Shay must have gone back to sleep.

With the greatest care, she turned the knob of the door. It was unlocked. As she nimbly opened it without the least noise, heated air wafted toward her. This room, too, had a fireplace in it where cheerful flames flickered in the grate.

Then she saw the great beast of a dog peering at her with mistrust. He was a massive creature—no doubt he weighed more than she did. However, Ula did not fear animals, she had no reason to do so. Without exception, they all obeyed her. She stared back at the dog and he came to her with his huge mouth split into a happy grin.

Close your mouth. Be quiet. Follow me. She gave her instructions with her thoughts.

The dog obeyed her commands and padded out of the bedroom. She sighed remembering that men were not as easy to command as animals were. Then again, perhaps the difficulty arose due to the volatile nature of the male species. She wished she could have encountered a few testosterone-driven individuals before last night's fiasco. It might have given her an understanding of how to manage them.

Balor happened to be a druid, a fact that sent a chill icing her veins. If she had a difficult time controlling ordinary men, what would it be like when she came face to face with the master wizard?

Trying to rid herself of that frightening prospect, she turned and shot a glance at the sleeping form on the bed. A blanket lay draped low over Shay's hips affording her a most intriguing view. Thoughts of Balor vanished from her mind as her gaze caught and held the sight of Shay's naked back. She had studied countless photographs of men wearing bathing suits and briefs, but none of those pictures had ever affected her. Staring at Shay's back, she found a curious swooping sensation in her nether regions, which confused her.

Transfixed by the well-defined muscles in his shoulders and the manner in which his torso narrowed at his hips, she found a thirst coming over her that had nothing to do with a drink of water.

Men were altogether different creatures from women, and the sight of Shay's bare flesh fascinated her. In one abrupt motion, he rolled over, and she knew a moment of panic, but he did not open his eyes. As her alarm subsided, she feasted on the view of his solid chest and the curling mat of hair that tapered downward well below his navel. She knew what remained hidden beneath the blanket's folds. She had read about a man's sexual organ and seen a scientific diagram in a medical book.

A princess must submit to her husband's needs. Meara had not gone into much detail on that matter. Then again, Meara had never been married. Ula had seen animals mate in the wilds of the Pine Barrens. For animals, it all appeared to be a relatively quick procedure. Could it be like that for people, too?

She could barely contain herself. Should she dare a peek? A low whine behind her drew her attention. She turned once more to the dog and focused on him.

Be still and wait.

The dog rigidly obeyed.

On her tiptoes, Ula hurried across the floor. Her fingers itched with the need to run her touch along the wide expanse of Shay's firmly ridged skin, still bronzed from last summer's sun.

Well aware she might wake him, she lifted the corner of the blanket covering him with painstaking care to move it away from his hips. She stifled a gasp when she saw that most curious object of a man's sex. Nestled in a soft tangle of brown hair, it did not appear as fearsome as the one she had seen in the medical textbook. That strange picture had displayed a cut-away view detailing the tissues within the appendage. The fact that it could change, growing large and stiff when the time came for mating caused her some trepidation. How big would it get, she wondered?

Swallowing hard, she thought of her own small self. The idea of getting married and submitting to her husband's needs frightened her—even though as a princess she was brave— most of the time. Certainly, she found it easy to be fearless when she could command any creature to do her will, but after discovering that at times men were the notable exception her unease about the marriage act weighed on her mind.

No doubt, when she married, her husband would find ways to keep his eyes averted, and she might be easily overpowered. The strength she had discovered in Shay's arms had surprised her, and intimidated her. An odd shudder went through her as she remembered what it had been like to be in his arms, to feel his strong heart pounding against her palm and to breathe in the scent of him. He had stirred feelings in her that left her nearly breathless.

She shook her head to try and force the memory to some far corner of her mind. She knew nothing about the world other than what she had read in books, magazines, and catalogs. She had grown up hidden in the bog in the pine forest for her safety.

She knew nothing about men and she had never met any of them until last night.

Leaving her home in the bog to marry a stranger and bear his children—to submit to his *needs,* did not sound like much fun. Especially, since she wanted to see more of the world than simply the catalogs she had feasted on for years. Still, she had been told that she must fulfill her destiny. Meara had hinted that chaos would result otherwise.

Drat. Destiny sounded so *fatal!*

Ula sighed and moved the blanket to cover Shay's lower region. She fought against the urge to touch his magnificent body, to feel the warmth of his skin against hers. She could see the throbbing pulse in his neck and it seemed she felt an echoing thump in her own body. The heat in the room became oppressive. Perspiration beaded on her upper lip, and she licked it away with her tongue.

Then, as suddenly as before, the terrible noise exploded in the room. A cacophony of intensity, with drums and such wailing as she never had heard in her lifetime. The noise came from a small black box beside the bed. Did a demon inhabit the box? Was Shay in league with a terrible fiend? Had he brought her to his house only to capture her in an evil plan?

The clamor started an ache in her ears. Covering them, she turned to flee. That's when the dreadful commotion ended. A strong arm grabbed her about the waist and pulled her down, impeding her flight.

"What are you doing in my room?"

He had her on his lap--directly above his naked .... She gulped but reassured herself that it was not ... ready. Still, she found she could barely breathe as her pulse's maddening pace left her dizzy. His voice sounded rough and every hair on her head trembled of its own accord. She knew she could never escape his grasp. The man had muscles as hard as the wood of an oak.

"Take your hands off me!" she demanded, swallowing her fear. *A princess is always firm with subordinates.* "What demon do you have in that box?"

Chapter Three

If Shay had believed her to be daft last night, in the gray light of the new morning, he thought he might need to call 911. The woman did not make much sense at all. He did not let her go.

"That is WIFO, and though it might sound like demonic music, it is very good at waking me up in the morning." The hint of violets still lingering in her hair teased his nostrils. He glanced toward the down jacket he had thrown over the chair last night. His pants, folded beneath the jacket, appeared not to have been disturbed--which meant she had probably not taken his wallet. Maybe. She could be one of those crooks with very light fingers.

He cast his gaze around the room. Where was Bran? Bran should have warned him that an interloper had invaded his bedroom. Dumb dog.

"Can the demon get out?" she whispered.

He heard a slight quiver in her voice. "Out?"

"Of that box?"

"The radio?"

"*That's* a radio?" Something like awe edged into her tone. "But it doesn't look like the one in the JC Penney catalog." She squirmed in his lap.

He held back a groan as he realized his precarious situation. Dammit. He did not need a lap dance from her this morning. "My radio came from Best Buy." He held her still while with his free hand, he felt her forehead for lumps. "Did you hit your head when you fell against the table last night?" His hand slid through some of the mass of wavy red hair. As the strands ran through his fingers, every one of them appeared to glow with fire though it had merely been touched by the morning's uncertain dawn streaming down from the skylight above his bed. The action sparked the flames of desire in him.

"No." Her breathy answer did nothing to ease the heat surging in his veins. "That brew I drank last night made my brain a wee bit muddled though."

Forcing himself to remove his hand from her hair, he tried

to eliminate his errant thoughts. "Aye, you were smashed."

"The only smashing I saw was your fist plowing into that man's nose!"

Shay winced. He had never used his hands in such a destructive manner. To be truthful, his fist was a bit sore and swollen.

"If I hadn't hit him, he would have hit me," he said. "But you're the one who caused all the chaos. What are you doing in my room anyway?" He could not help but be suspicious of her.

He felt her muscles tense even through the layer of soft green velvet. Unfortunately, her action stimulated him. He clenched his teeth.

"I--I heard your dog bark and I thought he might be hungry."

Shay glanced around. "Did you let him out?"

"No. I told him to wait."

Shay frowned. The wolfhound had failed obedience classes. His dog was a singular minded animal who felt he was equal--or better--than any human and therefore did not pay much attention to commands from anyone. To Bran, life was for fun. "Did he obey you?"

"Of course. He is still waiting."

He did not believe her. How could he? He knew Bran--who at this very moment was probably lying on the couch because he had been forbidden to do so.

With some reluctance and a great deal of restraint, Shay released Ula from his grasp. Holding her on his lap--especially in his current state of undress--had been a rash move. Simply touching her, and enduring the gentle aroma of violets imbued in her skin turned him on. He wanted nothing more than to unbutton the back of her dress--or better yet, lift up her skirt. That idea sent his personal bonfire sizzling to the point of combustion.

"The dog food is in the cabinet. If you'll be good enough to pour some in Bran's bowl and give him some fresh water, I'll get some clothes on." *I need a cold shower, too,* he admitted to himself. He gripped her with both hands to set her on her feet. His hands nearly spanned her small waist. With a supreme force of will he merely patted her backside to shoo her away from him. Before she turned to face him, he grabbed more blanket. Dammit. He did not need this kind of excitement.

"What does the dog food look like?"Her fingers twisted into a knot.

"It's the dry dog food in the bag."

"Oh. In a bag."

"It's a large bag. You can't miss it."

"All right then. Bran will have some breakfast."

"I'll fix you up some eggs in a few minutes."

"That would be so kind of you, sir."

"Shay. Don't you remember my name?"

"Yes, of course. 'Tis such a soft name, as I said last night."

Good. She had some recollection of the past evening's events. He noticed her gaze focused on a section of his anatomy considerably lower than his face. He could feel the burn rising up his neck.

Bran gave a loud, pitiful whine. Ula cleared her throat, but made no move to leave the room.

"Bran. Is. Hungry." He emphasized each word in an effort to get through to her. "I'll be thanking you to close the door of my room as you leave."

She blinked as if he had startled her. "Yes. Of course. The poor creature."

He heard her take in a great gulp of air before she raced out of the room muttering something that had the word "princess" in it.

When he heard the click of the lock, he wiped the sweat from his brow. At least she hadn't mentioned the bulge in the blanket. He could not believe he had reacted like that, especially to a woman who appeared more than a little balmy.

Can the demon get out? She acted as if she had never seen a radio until now, other than the one in the JC Penney catalog.

He was thinking maybe she had spent a lot of time in a padded cell.

He grabbed the pants from the chair and reached in to check his wallet. Nothing had been removed. Breathing a sigh of relief, he stumbled into the bathroom and flicked on the light without thinking. The light did not go on. Power had not been restored. He wondered how long it would take for the electricity to return. Good thing his clock radio had a battery backup. He wondered if he should have bought a generator for his other appliances.

Then an even more troubling question came to mind. How soon could he get Ula off his hands? With the height of the snow, it might take a while to make the roads passable. He would get out his snow thrower and clear his own driveway, but the plows had to come through town before he could return Ula to wherever she belonged.

He stepped into the large claw-footed tub that had come with the house. Drawing the shower curtain around the tub, he turned on the water. The hot water tank had retained some heat, but not much. The tepid water in the cool bathroom felt like icy needles stinging his skin. Nevertheless, the chill stream gushing out did alleviate the throbbing desire that had come upon him with such a vengeance.

Oddly enough, he regretted washing away the scent of her. He had recognized the hint of old-fashioned violets immediately--a perfume few modern women wore. His mother had coaxed dainty violet plants to grow in her garden. He remembered the heavy cakes of soap bearing the same aroma tucked into drawers in the little cottage where he had grown up. A touch of homesickness swept over him with an ache that made his throat close up.

Toweling off quickly, he pulled on a pair of clean sweats, intent on fixing something to eat--and soon.

"Ula?" He stepped into the living room and glanced toward the fireplace. Her socks and boots had been removed from their place on the hearth. There was no sign of her cloak either.

He clenched his jaw. And where was his dog?

"Bran!" he shouted. "Bran! Where are you boy?"

A muffled whine came from the garage. Whirling, Shay raced toward the door that led to the garage. Throwing it open, he halted for a moment as confusion warred against the rage inside him. Ula had fashioned a simple sled out of some spare lumber he had in the garage. She had whipped the boards together with rope. Very clever.

Inside the sled sat Bran and his entire bag of dog food. Ula had snowshoes strapped to her boots.

"Where do you think you're going?" He covered the distance between them in three long strides while holding his fists rigidly at his sides.

"Why... I was taking the dog for a walk." She smiled back at him.

A strange sensation take hold of him, as if a vacuum latched onto his brain and started sucking out memories. He shook his head to clear it.

Then he remembered what she had said last night. *I've a need for a dog--to help with some hunting.*

"You're stealing my dog!" He snatched at the leash trailing from Bran's collar. He unhooked it from the rope attached to the sled.

She drew herself up, giving the appearance of affronted dignity. "I intended to return him. As I told you last night, I must have a dog. It is a matter of life or death."

"Then call the FBI!" Despite the anger pumping through him, he noticed that even wearing boots and snowshoes she barely came up to the bottom of his chin. His errant thoughts returned to how lovely she looked... how little she weighed... how small her waist felt in his hands.

"I've read about the FBI, but they would be of little use. Dogs have a keen sense of smell, and can be trained."

"You keep your hands off my dog!" He growled with as much force as he could muster while considering that her lips reminded him of the raspberry jam in a holiday trifle. He ran his tongue along the edge of his mouth as if he could almost taste the sweetness.

Bran gave a small whimper and licked his hand without

the usual enthusiasm. Shay frowned at his pet as a small curl of fear wound around his heart. "What have you done to my dog?"

"Nothing." She did not flinch despite his accusation. "I merely asked him to help me, and he agreed."

Shay rubbed his hand across his forehead. Now she believed she could talk to his dog. Nothing about her made any sense, but indeed the simple sight of her kindled a desire so hot he could use another cold shower.

"Bran, what's the matter, boy?" He knelt beside his dog and massaged the animal's soft coat.

Bran perked up, wagged his tail, and gave a happy bark.

"There. You see no harm's been done. By the saints, there's nothing the matter with your dog."

He did not trust her. Grabbing the bag of dog food, he held it in front of him to hide the evidence of his lust. "If you want to leave here now, that's fine with me, but you'll be noticing that the roads aren't plowed and the snow is deep. It's quite a hike back to town from here, but believe me, I won't be stopping you."

When she lowered her head, he felt like a beast. He couldn't allow her to walk out. She could drown in some of the drifts. Letting her attempt a trek back to town under the current conditions would be irresponsible--even criminal.

The quiver in her ragged sigh softened some of the hardness in his heart. However, it made another part of him far firmer. He turned around and headed back to the kitchen. "If you're hungry, I'll be making some breakfast."

Bran whined and tugged at the leash as if he wanted to stay in the garage.

Shay glared at the dog. "What do you want? Bacon?"

Bran whined again and looked from Ula to Shay and back again.

"All right. Is sausage an acceptable bribe today?" Shay grumbled.

Bran gave one happy bark and raced toward the door, dragging Shay along in his wake.

"Aye. The way to a dog's heart is through his stomach."

Shay wished Bran would ignore Ula, but the dog had developed an instant attachment for her. In fact, Ula seemed to have no problem getting everyone to kowtow to her whims-- except him.

Nevertheless, the impact she had on him could only be compared to an earthquake. Maybe her mind was messed up, but it came in a very nice package. He could not ignore her hair, her body, her toes, her fingers, and the lilt in her voice. Everything about her turned him on.

He stared out the window as he cracked open the eggs to prepare breakfast. Dammit. He could not think straight, and she surely had a bit of mischief on her mind.

Then he remembered one more *geise* and a cold finger slid down his spine. *Thou shalt not refuse a woman the company of your dog.*

He clenched his teeth. *No! I will not allow her to steal my dog.* Why must his father's old ideas haunt him? Why should some old rules have any effect on his life?

Ula entered the kitchen and ambled around asking him questions.

"This is a microwave. Right?" She patted it like she patted Bran--rather lovingly--and he wondered if she would toss the appliance in her sled, too, given the chance.

He grunted in reply.

"This is a refrigerator. Right?" She put her hand on the handle.

"Do not open that!"

"Why not?"

"Because we don't have any power."

She ran her hands along the sides of the refrigerator. "You opened it and took out the eggs."

"I opened it briefly."

"Oh." Her fine brows lifted, revealing those eerie eyes of hers. Shay felt some chord vibrate in him whenever he glanced at her eyes. As far as he was concerned, her eyes should be licensed as lethal weapons. He ought to hand her a pair of sunglasses.

"I'd recognize a coffee maker anywhere." She traced the

manufacturer's name emblazoned on the machine. "I'd love a cup of coffee."

"There is no power!" He found his temper rising, but that was infinitely better than finding his sweat pants too tight in one specific area.

"You keep mentioning that. What kind of power do you mean?"

"Electric power."

"Oh! I read about that. Thomas Edison opened the first power station in New York."

"Correct."

"So... why do you have all these machines if you have no power?"

Shay stopped stirring the eggs and peered at her. Maybe he should call up the hospital and ask them if they were missing a psych patient. "Somewhere a line went down due to the snow."

"A line...."

"A power line. It brings the electricity to the house."

"But your radio worked."

"It has a back-up battery."

"Then why don't you get one of those for the coffee maker? I would love a cup of coffee."

The pull of her gaze tugged at him, like a magnet … drawing him .... He shut his eyes. Opening them again, he stared at the bowl of eggs. He had almost forgotten he was supposed to be scrambling up some food. He cleared his throat.

"You'll not be getting coffee this morning. Maybe tea if I can get the water boiling in the fireplace." He poured the eggs into a pan and walked into the living room to cook them over the fire.

Kneeling by the hearth, he held the pan over the flames. "I hope you like your eggs scrambled." If there was a touch of sarcasm in his tone, she didn't seem to notice.

"Scrambled eggs would be heavenly. Indeed, I am not a fussy eater and chicken eggs are my favorite."

Chicken eggs? Shay shrugged as he stirred the eggs with a

spatula. So maybe she was a connoisseur and had tried ostrich eggs. Or duck eggs.

He turned to see her sitting at the table in the kitchen patting Bran on the head. The dog had never appeared so content, which irked Shay.

Her tapestry bag sat beside her on the floor. How had she hidden snowshoes in it? Where were her snowshoes now? Had she left them in the garage, ready for her next escape with his dog? His nerves tensed and he pressed his jaw firmly together.

With a sudden clunk, the damper slid shut. Shay had no time for panic. He snatched up the poker to pry the damper open again before too much smoke filled the room.

Choking on the smoke, with his eyes stinging he swore. "That blasted damper should not close by itself!" The damper refused to budge as he struggled with it. After bellowing out a string of curses, he roared, "I built this chimney!"

* * * *

Ula clicked her tongue. Sure and it was bad enough for smoke to be billowing out of the fireplace, but Shay had to go and use such abominable language in her presence. The man needed a talking to. Shaking her head, she hurried into the garage where she had seen a bucket filled with sand. Lugging it back into the house, she set the heavy bucket by the hearth and scooped out handfuls of sand as Shay continued wrestling with the damper.

In a matter of minutes, she had extinguished the fire. "You should always keep the bucket of sand next to the fireplace."

He let out another string of foul language as he sat back on his heels and wiped his sooty brow with his hand.

"You're not to talk that way in my presence--or in the presence of any lady." She put her hands on her hips and glared at him.

The vexation on his face matched the irritation in his voice. "I'll thank you for putting out the fire, but I'll not be minding my P's and Q's for you."

Every nerve in her body tensed when yet again he did not obey her. Bewildered and somewhat shaken by his resistance to her commands, she nibbled on her lip. She had been staring straight into his eyes--and his gaze had been directed at her. He should completely agree with her.

"I can't understand why that damper slammed shut," he went on. "That shouldn't have happened."

A quiver traced through her veins. Meara had always told Ula that her power would work on everyone, without exception. What if Balor ignored her command, too?

She put a hand to her forehead. Perhaps, it was the headache behind her eyes that had distracted her focus. She really should have something to eat. Her stomach did not feel as nauseous as it had earlier. Swallowing her nervousness, she knelt beside Shay on the hearth. Trying to shake off her unease, she lifted up the pan of blackened eggs using the edge of her velvet skirt to protect her hand. "I'm thinking you've ruined this batch of eggs. Do you have oats?"

"Aye. And there are still some sausages." He got to his feet. "I've got to open the windows to let out the smoke."

"Then I'll be making our breakfast." She gave him a smile even as she felt plagued by doubts. While he continued to try and solve the problem with the damper, she fixed up a pot of oats, some sausages, and hot tea using the other fireplace in his bedroom. By the time she had the table set, he thought he had the problem with the damper solved.

"A faulty pin," he explained as he washed up in the sink. "The constant heat must have cracked it. I've replaced it and it should work fine now but the manufacturer should be using a better grade of steel."

As they sat to eat at the table, she found her appetite had vanished, but she knew she had to force down the food. She needed strength to save Meara. She hardly tasted the fine meal she had prepared, though it appeared as if Shay enjoyed every morsel for he wolfed it down without even an attempt at polite conversation.

Her emotions churned inside her. How could she get the dog away from him? More importantly, what would she do if the dog could not locate Meara? Or worse, what if she found Meara too late?

Smoothing down the crumpled green velvet of her skirt,

she thought of the many hours she and Meara had spent sewing the luxurious fabric in the expectant hope of the arrival of the dark-eyed man who would take her away from the bog as foretold at her birth. Only Meara knew the man's lineage, but in true druidic fashion she had not written down the particulars. She had committed it to memory.

Without Meara, Ula would never be able to fulfill her destiny. Without Meara, Ula would be forced to remain in the bog indefinitely. Waiting. Staring at the pictures in her catalogs.

She dared a glance at Shay. He sat at the opposite end of the table wearing a tight, short- sleeved shirt that revealed his wide shoulders and massive biceps. He did not look up at her.

She studied the short hair covering his forearms, which extended onto the back of his hands. She peered at her own two hands, not a single hair grew there. On her arms, the fine downy hair could barely be discerned due to the pale color of it.

When she had risen from his lap in the bedroom, she had seen the bulge beneath the blanket. Awareness that his appendage must have swelled to a much larger size had sent shivers racing up and down her spine. Thinking about the event now as she watched him eat, created a swirl of anticipation in her. Obviously, a man could be ready for the sexual act in as much time as it took to run a comb through but one section of her hair.

The thoughts she had about him sent such tremors through her that she became aware of a dampness at that very secret place of her sex.

"Don't you like the sausages?" he asked, piercing her with his deep blue eyes.

"I-I'm quite full. I haven't eaten such a grand breakfast in quite a while. I don't think I could fit in another bite," she added in a whisper.

Let me borrow your dog. She focused on him with more intensity than she had ever had to use, but it did no good. Instead, she found herself filled with a heat that made her limbs weak and warmed her cheeks.

"You're still angry, aren't you?" he taunted. "Too bad. You'll not be stealing my dog. That's a fine way to pay me back for taking you in last night. I should have left you in the pub to fend for yourself."

Ula lowered her head and stared at her plate. The memory of that bagpiper kissing her had her stomach sloshing about in a disturbing manner. She lifted her napkin and pressed it against her lips. If only she could erase that memory and the panic she had felt.

"Hey. I'm sorry." Shay's voice held a note of repentance. "I would never have left you with that brute."

She took an unsteady breath and tried to regain some control of her emotions. "I'm-- that's--." She lifted her head. *Please loan me your dog for a few hours.*

"Next time, don't ask a drunken man to buy you a meal."

"Aye. I'll remember." While she could not understand why Shay did not respond to her commands, she could plainly see the suspicion he harbored for her. As she would be forced to use trickery against him, he had every right to mistrust her. She reminded herself that there could be no other way.

He lifted one corner of his mouth and shook his head as if he pitied her. "And don't drink more than you can handle."

A dark sense of despair ripped through her. She realized that in his own way, Shay had been kind to her--far kinder than she deserved.

Nevertheless, she had to save Meara. If the druidess was beside her right now, she would know the reason Shay did not obey her commands. Then she would create a spell forcing him to succumb to Ula's wishes, but Meara could not help her. Ula was all alone.

Swallowing past the ache in her throat, she accepted the fact that she had no options. Bran remained her best hope. She decided to try a different strategy.

"I had a dog once." She reached into the bag to pull out a sketch. "We named him Lugh." She pushed the sketch toward him. "I missed him so much after he died. He was a stray-- nothing like your fine pet."

He shoved the sketch away, slapped his hands on the table

and stood up. "I'm sorry about your dog, but you'll not be taking mine."

She quailed when she saw his nostrils widen with fury, but in an instant, the atmosphere in the room changed and the air became charged with a different type of tension. His jaw tightened, the pulse throbbed in his neck, and his gaze raked over her. She bit back a gasp. The depths of his eyes glittered with need--a need that had everything to do with her. She could tell by the growing protrusion in his pants. What strange creatures men were!

More mysterious were the changes going on within her own body. The yearning ache blossoming in her nether regions gnawed like an insatiable hunger.

She knew she should run from him, but she could hardly tear her gaze away. Excitement filled her with anticipation as she drank in the hazy wonder of the lust-laden atmosphere.

Without warning, he turned away and broke the mood. "I want to get you back to wherever you belong as quickly as possible so I am going to clear the driveway--and Bran will be with me. If you steal anything from this house in the meantime, I will not hesitate to call the police and press charges."

"Steal?" A chill slid through her as all the excitement of a moment before faded away. "I have no need for any common baubles." *What I want is you!*

How could he build up such a fierce passion within her with the mere thought of his readiness for intimacy, but then shut his own desires off as easily as one snuffed out a candle?

Ula never experienced rejection until now and it hurt, though the warmth in her belly lingered. Surely the sex act in humans--or submitting as Meara had called it--could not be as simple as the brief and common rutting of animals. She had hoped for more when her time came to submit-- though the brief way Meara had discussed it gave her the impression that it was a rather distasteful deed.

Ula ached for Shay's touch. He could not do this to her! She would die of ... of frustration! She moved toward him, watching him run his hand through his soft brown hair. His shoulders flexed and she wanted to touch them, to feel the ripples of his hard sinews as they bunched into a tight knot. Then she wanted to go further—and touch--well, all of him-- but especially the part that had intrigued her as he had lain asleep.

Coming from behind, she reached out to lay one hand upon his forearm. He stiffened.

"Don't try to tell me how honest you are. You've been trying to kidnap Bran from the moment you found out about him. I know I can't trust you."

The rough hairs on his arm rubbed against her palm and started a perilous current stirring in her veins. Her other arm snaked around his waist as she leaned her head against his back. She heard the thunder of his heart, and her own pulse leaped in response. Breathing in the scent of him added to the flood of emotions whirling through her.

She forgot about the dog. For the moment, she even forgot about Meara. Every thought, every nerve in her body focused on Shay, on his wonderful body and the pleasure coursing through her as she clung to him. She wanted to caress more of his skin, she longed to be even closer.

Sliding her hand underneath his shirt, she closed her eyes and gave into the sensation of touching his hot flesh. She sighed, starving for so much more.

"Stop it. I know what you're trying to do." He growled out the words with such ferocity, she flinched and drew back. Would he be turning into a pooka as in one of Meara's old tales? Fear settled like a cold stone inside her.

"I'll be having none of what you're offering and certainly I'll not be trading my dog for it." He stamped away from her. "You can get busy cleaning up the table and washing the dishes." With that he yanked a coat off a hook by the door and called to Bran. The dog gave her a mournful look and whined.

"Bran. Come," he snarled.

Shay's sharp words sliced her heart. Meara could be a stern disciplinarian, but she never failed to remind Ula that she loved her.

Shay did not love her. And why should he? After all, she

did intend to take his dog, though for the very best of reasons. She bit her lip to hold in her emotions. Gathering her thoughts as best she could, she gazed at the dog. *Go along with your master. You and I will romp in the snow later.*

Bran smiled and gave a single bark before he followed his master into the garage.

Easing herself down into a chair, Ula was mystified by the consuming sense of want Shay had awakened in her. She had never realized that she--a princess--possessed such a strong driving passion. Only Shay's denial kept her from going further, though he could not hide the fact that he desired her as much as she ached for him. However, he was capable of turning off his feelings. She was not, and since he did not respond to her commands, she would have to accept the situation.

She searched her conscience to see if she could remember any of Meara's instructions concerning the sexual act, but as usual she came up with very little. Meara had been rather close- mouthed on the topic in general.

Ula's heart felt a painful squeeze. She could wind up spending the rest of her life in the bog--alone! How could she live with this terrible unsatisfied emotion?

That is--unless Balor came for her and captured her by some trickery. She covered her eyes and shook her head, feeling crushed by the hopelessness of her future destiny. If only Shay's eyes were not blue. There was not the slightest chance that he could ever be her husband. Still, she had been surprised that he had thought she wanted to coerce him into sex so she could steal his dog. That idea had not occurred to her at all. She had simply been swept away by the power of her yearning.

Drumming her fingers on the table, she thought about what it would be like to share Shay's love. While he seemed to be completely unaffected by her thoughts, she could distract him--at least momentarily--with her touch. She wished she knew more about men. Whatever knowledge she had gained of the strange creatures had come to her from books she had read. She needed a manual on how to deal with a man--or, at least, how to deal with Shay.

Of course, once she ran away with his dog he would have every right to hate her. Her eyes misted. She truly did not want to hurt him, but what could she do? She had to save Meara.

No doubt, Shay would do his best to track her down. The thought sent an odd surge of panic sweeping through her. No one must know the location of her hidden *bothy*. Ever. Meara had been quite clear on that point. Ula's future husband was supposed to find her anyway. Meara considered that part of the test of his true love.

To Ula, it made no sense at all.

With trembling fingers she opened Meara's tapestry bag and squelched the sob that threatened to rise up in her throat. All she had left of Meara right now was her magic. What would she do if that was all she would ever have? She began to pull out Meara's decoctions, tinctures, herbs, and the other implements necessary for the spells that Meara used. How she wished there was a spell that could bring the druidess back instantly.

Then she closed her eyes and thought of Shay. What if she would never see him again? Fisting her hands, she wondered how her feelings for Shay could be so strong when he was literally the first man she had ever met.

Opening her eyes, she prayed for the strength to keep from collapsing into a well of despair. She straightened her back and reminded herself that she had a destiny to fulfill, but first, she must find Meara. Right now, that was all that really mattered, but somehow--some way, she promised herself that she would see Shay again as well.

Chapter Four

Shay glanced around the garage. He did not see any snowshoes. Where had that woman put them? He checked a few places where she might have hidden them, but the snowshoes seemed to have vanished. Muttering a few curses, he rolled the snow thrower out of the garage.

A gusty wind bit at his skin but he hardly noticed. The audacity of that woman still had him reeling. Angry at his own body for reacting to her touch, he wanted to rid himself of the hormones she had stirred up. He intended to push the snow thrower and his body to the limits. He cursed himself for being so tenderhearted and bringing her home so she wouldn't get into any more trouble.

Then he thought of her small waist, those delicate feet of hers, that fiery hair--the softness of her flesh when he had held her, the hint of violets that swirled about her, the tender valley between her breasts ....

Bran whimpered and derailed Shay's obsessive train of thought. That woman could send *him* to the psych ward. Glancing at his pet, he noted how miserable the animal appeared.

"You're supposed to be a courageous dog. I'm wanting to see you laugh at the weather."

Bran whined.

"I'll not have a wimpy dog," Shay complained. "Or one that lets crazy women steal them away."

Bran hung his head in utter wretchedness.

"Serves you right for falling in love with her," Shay chastised the dog. "Do you think it's going to be fun hunting in this weather? And what is she hunting for? Have you asked her that?"

He should have asked her. No. He should have run in the other direction.

He should have listened to the *geise.* It made a lot of sense not to bring a woman into the house. Right now, Ula could be helping herself to ....

He stopped to think a moment. She seemed inordinately

interested in his appliances, but aside from those work-saving devices he did not own anything worth stealing--except for his tools and his dog-- and his truck. Judging from the fiasco in the pub, she did not have a license. Odd.

Shay cranked the knob so that the chute would throw the snow to the right side of the driveway. Then he yanked on the cord to start the snow thrower. Nothing happened. Swearing, he gave it another pull, but the engine refused to turn over. It had gas in it. It had been working last week. It had a brand new spark plug in it. There should not be anything wrong with it.

In a fury, he pulled again on the cord—and again until his arm burned from the exertion.

"Dammit!" He cursed as he rolled the snow thrower back into the garage and got out a snow shovel. Still enraged, he pitched the shovel into the first snowdrift and the handle snapped in two.

Shay stared at it in disbelief. Bran let out a howl and the sound cut through Shay like a fine blade.

...misfortune and even death.

"I am cursed is it?" He asked his dog as he stumbled back against the wall of his house. "Doomed because I have broken one of my *geise*. Doomed because I won't let her have my dog."

Bran let out another howl and scratched at the door.

"You'd leave me here to my death?" he asked his pet. "After I've trained you, fed you, cared for you and paid so much money for the vet bills that I know the doctor could not have purchased his Porsche without my business!"

Bran whined and scratched at the door once more.

Shay stared out at the solid white landscape and felt his heart sinking. Somehow, it did seem as if the *geise* was working against him. It did not make any sense, but there could be no other explanation. The damper should not have slammed shut. The snow thrower should be working. That snow shovel had a lifetime guarantee.

He brightened as an idea formed in his mind. Opening the door of the garage for Bran he decided that anything was worth a try under the circumstances. He did not need any more broken dampers, non-working snow throwers, or broken snow shovels. He would end the curse of this *geise* the way he had handled the other one last night--in a devious manner.

* * * *

Ula had half of the kitchen table littered with an assortment of Meara's decoctions, tinctures, dried herbs, and other implements. The druidess had carefully labeled each bottle, though she never wrote down any of her incantations. Those she kept secure by filing them away in her memory— where every word would be forever lost if Ula did not succeed in locating her.

Over the years, Ula spent a great deal of time listening to Meara recite some of her everyday magic--and a few times, Ula tried some spells on her own--when Meara wasn't looking. However, none of those chants ever turned out right. She knew it was a matter of the proper inflection, but though she tried, she never succeeded.

Meara caught her after her last attempt, which resulted in a spectacular disaster. It took half the day for Meara to rectify the mess Ula had made.

"You are a princess, not a druidess." Meara warned her never to play with magic again.

Until now, Ula had kept her word. Sighing, she dug deeper into the tapestry bag and pulled out a red candle. Then she noticed a pin amongst the clutter on the table. Not long ago, she remembered Meara casting a love spell for her friend who often came to visit. Meara's friend was the one who had given Ula so many fine catalogs like the JC Penney one she enjoyed most of all.

Ula recalled the simple steps for the love spell. It seemed harmless enough--a simple, straightforward charm, not a complicated incantation where one slip of a syllable could be downright catastrophic. How much could go wrong with a love spell? If it worked, maybe Shay would love her--and always remember her with fondness even if he could never be her husband.

If it softened his attitude toward her just the slightest bit maybe he wouldn't shout at her or use vile language in her presence ... maybe he wouldn't turn away from her ... maybe he would let her touch him. If a little enchantment gave her only a small amount of influence ... for certainly her own power had no effect on him... maybe he would loan the dog to her without a fuss.

Still, guilt weighed on her as she picked up the pin and wrote her name along with Shay's name on the candle. Frowning, she searched through the assortment of bottles on the table until she found rose oil. She opened the bottle and sniffed. The aroma of summer's wild roses set her pulse racing.

Spilling a few drops on the candle, she used her fingers to rub the oil into the wax. Shay kept matches next to the fireplace, and she had seen a candleholder there as well. She fetched those items and after placing the candle in the holder, she lit the wick. A peculiar tingling danced through her, and then a warmth spread throughout her body. Her breasts grew heavy while a languorous debility settled into her limbs, making her long to lie down--on Shay's bed. A touch of alarm wound through her as the overpowering yearning gnawed at her, craving satisfaction. She took a deep breath and pressed her hands upon her midriff, as if she could hold the feelings at bay. She had not realized the charm would have such a disconcerting effect on *her*. Uneasy, she reassured herself that anything was worth a try under the circumstances.

As she started to place some of Meara's paraphernalia back into the tapestry bag, Shay entered the kitchen with Bran trotting behind him. When she glanced up to see the wide grin on Shay's face, she felt the blood drain from her own. His smile bore all the triumph of a conqueror.

Ula could barely breathe. The charm shouldn't work that fast! She tried to stare into his eyes and command him.

You will have no lustful thoughts! Naturally, his grin did not fade. She could only assume her order did not work. She wondered if it could be due to the difficulty she had trying to rein in her own immodest ideas.

She watched his gaze roam downward, one seductive millimeter at a time from her face to her breasts. She knew she should be annoyed with his supreme arrogance--even if she had initiated the love charm, but his bold assessment only served to turn her insides into a sweet mound of warm pudding.

"I've something to say to you." His husky voice vibrated through her, setting off small earthquakes near her thighs.

Her pulse raced as she blew out the candle, hoping that would put a stop to the magic. With one arm, she scooped all of Meara's things back into the bag--including the candle.

Shay took off his coat and tossed it onto the back of one of the chairs. Then he slid into the seat beside Ula and rested his forearms on the table so he could stare into her face. Her heart lurched with excitement, and she found herself nearly lightheaded from the tension.

"I'll let you go hunting with my dog if you pay me seventy-five dollars an hour and I am allowed to go along with you."

"Seventy-five dollars!" Complete panic gripped her. "I don't have that much money!"

"That clasp on your cloak is solid gold. Where did you steal it?"

Stunned, her mouth gaped open in horror. What had she done? Meara had warned her. She had failed again, unable to manage even a simple charm. Shay didn't like her any better than he had before--in fact, he thought she was a common criminal.

"My parents gave me that clasp. It's important and I must never lose it." *Especially now, when I'll be meeting Balor, face to face.*

"Who are your parents?" His blue lobelia eyes narrowed.

She swallowed hard. If she told him who her parents were, he would not believe her. In fact, he might assume she was crazy.

"They're dead." Her lip quivered. She had never known her mother and father, but Meara had.

"Oh. I'm sorry." He lowered his head and drummed the table with his fingers for a moment. "Well, I'll be outside." Then he stood up, slipped into his coat, and walked back out the door. He did not call out to Bran, who lay on the floor.

She reached back into the tapestry bag and pulled out the candle. Trying to swallow the lump of sorrow in her throat, she snapped the candle in half--but the shameless feelings in her own body did not go away.

She sought to break the candle into even smaller pieces but she could not manage it. The rose oil had made the candle slippery. Rising from the table, she remembered the fireplace and dashed into the bedroom. She tossed the entire candle onto the fire. The minute the candle touched the flames, she knew she had only made matters worse. As the red wax melted and ignited, she sank down to the floor with the sudden blaze that raced through her. She thought she would be set afire, too. Drops of perspiration ran down her face. Moaning, she struggled to her feet and went back into the kitchen. She dug in the tapestry bag for a handkerchief to dab at her brow, but that did little good.

Rummaging around in the bag again, she found a fan, but it did not cool her skin. Desperate to find relief, she peeled off her heavy velvet gown. She stepped out of it and walked into Shay's bathroom. She turned on the faucets and filled the tub, adding a dollop of Meara's violet-scented bubbles. Stripping off the rest of her undergarments, she sank into the cold water only to discover the relief she sought would not be abated simply by bringing down the temperature of her skin.

* * * *

Convinced he had lost his mind, Shay blew great plumes of snow off the edge of the driveway with the snow thrower. At least telling Ula she could borrow his dog for a price had worked. The machine started right up with the first tug on the cord. However, simply talking to her stirred his body in ways he tried to deny by viciously attacking the snowdrifts in his driveway. Though the snow thrower balked at the height of the snow, Shay put all his weight behind the machine and moved relentlessly forward while trying to ignore the fire consuming him.

Despite the icy weather, he removed his coat but that did not help to cool him down. Sweat poured from his face as if he was in the middle of a summer heat wave. It didn't make any sense. The thermometer on the wall of his house registered thirty degrees. Not bad for the day after a blizzard, but he knew he should not be feeling so overheated.

On the return trip up the driveway, he had nearly reached the garage door when the snow thrower hit something, made a horrendous grinding noise, and stopped dead.

Shay froze. Was the *geise* still working against him? *...misfortune and even death.*

"No! I don't believe it!" He swore and backed the machine up a few feet so he could examine the cause of the machine's demise. Caught in the blades, he discovered a handsaw--his own handsaw--mangled by the snow thrower's blades. He would never be able to use that saw again, but even worse was the damage to the snow thrower. *If* it could be fixed, it would take time--and he wanted to be rid of Ula today.

Or did he? Her hair felt like silk, he enjoyed listening to her voice, and touching her waist had given him a reason to take a cold shower. He rubbed his brow. Yes, he needed to get her back to wherever she belonged. As soon as possible.

Overwhelmed by his seesawing emotions, he stared at the damage to the snow thrower and shook his head. How did his saw get outside in the snow? He always kept his tools in neat order in the garage. He would never leave them out in the weather.

Then he remembered the crude sled Ula had whipped together. Going back into the garage, he checked out her handiwork. The ends of the sled fit evenly together. Peering at the floor, he noticed a faint trail of sawdust. Following it, he found a pile of the stuff behind the broom in the corner of the garage.

The heat of desire he had been feeling a few minutes before detonated into rage. He stamped back into the house. Bran jumped up and then shrank away from Shay as he slammed the kitchen door. He paid scant attention to the dog. He went searching for Ula.

However, when he saw the pile of green velvet outside the bathroom door, his mouth went dry. His wrath veered off on a different course at the sight of that billowing gown lying in a discarded heap. His mind began racing with images of Ula without the dress, her breasts freed from the fabric, her delicate waist ... her legs ....

Once again, he grew hard. He could not fight it. What was the matter with him? He pounded on the door to the bathroom.

"Did you throw my handsaw out into the snow?"

"No." Her one breathy syllable had a fragile note in it.

"You used it!"

"Yes, but I did not put it into the snow."

"Then who else could have done it? Bran?" Sarcasm was not one of his better qualities.

"A demon ... perhaps ... would do such a thing."

For a grown woman to offer such a ridiculous solution only confirmed his suspicion that she was completely insane.

"You are the only other person in this house!" The unmistakable odor of violets wafted through the air, emanating from the small half-inch space underneath the door. The fragrance assailed him, siphoning away what was left of his reason. He forgot about the handsaw and the snow thrower. He wanted to see her--naked. He wanted to kiss her pale, violet-scented skin. He wanted to breathe in her fiery, violet-scented hair. He put his palms against the door and leaned his forehead on it. "What are you doing?"

"Taking ... a bath."

"There can't be any hot water left." He was hot--burning as much as a Fourth of July rocket. He needed to put out the fire.

"I--it is hot."

That made no sense, but his lust-fogged mind did not care. He stood outside the door, clinging to the few remnants of his sanity while visions of her in his huge claw-footed tub assaulted him. Overwhelmed, he could think of nothing else but drawing in enough air.

"Are you still there?" she asked.

He groaned.

"Please... come in."

From somewhere far back in his mind, alarm bells went

off. "What?"

"I need you."

"W-why?"

"Don't you feel it, too?"

"Hell." Of course, he felt it. From the moment he'd seen her in Paddy's Pub, he'd been fighting against his baser instincts and he knew he should continue to rein in his desires. The fast fading voice of reason warned him to turn around and walk away.

He ignored it. He opened the door to a hot and humid room where clouds of steam rose from the water. It was not possible. There was no power; therefore, there should be no hot water. He didn't care. He closed the door behind him.

She lay in the tub with her eyes closed and her head tilted back against the rim. The sight of her ripe, bare breasts floating amongst the scented bubbles sent a thunderbolt to Shay's core. As her breasts heaved with her breathing, he pulled his shirt over his head and tossed it to the floor.

"It's the charm. I cannot undo it." She gave a choked sob. "I thought it would be harmless."

He did not pay any attention to her words. After all, he figured she was demented and at the moment so was he. He should never have brought her home in the first place--but then he would never have seen her naked, perfect body in the tub. He slid out of his sweat pants and briefs in one smooth motion, freeing his hot arousal.

"When I threw the candle in the fire, I could think of nothing else but this aching for you."

He stepped into his commodious tub and sank in the scented bubbles. The water did nothing to ease the heat in his loins. Like a red-hot branding iron, his erection wanted only to burn into the tender folds of her deepest flesh.

She floated to him, her body atop his, her breasts pressed to his chest, her thighs alongside of his, her sweet folds brushing the firm fire of his sex.

"I'm sorry," she sobbed as her trembling arms circled his waist.

"Don't be." There was no need for an apology. All this

was madness--a nightmare--or an illusion that would vanish if he could thrust the hunger from his brain, but he could not--until he satiated his throbbing need.

He kissed her, crushing her lips to his. He did not believe a single word that came from those lips--everything she said was a bunch of blarney--but he was powerless to resist the urge to taste her. Wanting to devour every inch of her, he plunged into her mouth, where he found a sweet volcano waiting for him, which turned the blood in his veins into glowing lava.

As his tongue danced with hers, every part of his body burned with need. Nothing could cool him down save the release he knew he would find deep inside her dark, wet heat. He slid his hands down the length of her smooth, slippery skin and forgot about everything else except this woman who had driven him to the edge of madness.

* * * *

Every one of Ula's nerves felt singed as Shay drew his knees up and positioned her just above his hard hot sex. Pressing against it, she found herself nearly delirious, but he distracted her by drawing one rigid nipple into his mouth. His lips teased with cruel and deliberate torture, sending a sizzling spiral through her. She melted, becoming like the liquid surrounding her and flowing around Shay. Her hazy world became only the water and Shay. Last night, she had been drunk with strong liquor. Today she found herself in another foggy mist, but this was far, far worse. This time, she caused disaster not only for herself, but for Shay as well.

She moaned, but his fervent persecution continued until tidal waves of sensations surged through her. Far back in her mind, her persistent conscience insisted she should end this recklessness, but the power of the charm kept her at Shay's mercy. She gripped the edge of the tub as he floated her on her back and raised her buttocks with his knees so that he could feast on her inner thighs. His tongue delicately tasted her soft flesh, inching upward, creating a series of shivers that had her trembling with want. Then he reached her most private cleft, and his attack grew more insistent. Hard tremors stunned her as his tongue swept over her. Gasping for breath, she realized she had lost all control, but he became ever more relentless.

Desire consumed her, and she quivered with the power of her need. Never had she imagined that it would be like this--this unbearable passion that drove her to follow Shay's lead. He drew her hand down to touch the hard part of him that had so fascinated her that morning. A thrill went through her with the contact. Her fingers slid up and down its length, learning the shape, the size, and the feel of it--knowing that only this could satisfy the ache between her thighs.

His finger reached inside her and she found herself rocked by pulsating fire. He stoked her desire with his touch, adding fuel until she knew the torch inside her would ignite and she would be burned to ashes.

"I want you now," she pleaded.

"It is too soon." His harsh whisper singed her ear.

"Now." She writhed against him, unable to bear another moment of this maddening hunger.

Slowly, he drew her down upon his hot member. As she was filled with the heat of him, a searing pain startled her and a small gasp escaped her lips.

Shay's movement halted as his hands gripped her waist.

"I thought you ... you've never ...."

Did she see panic in his eyes? Or was it accusation? That she deserved, because she had caused this terrible ....

No. It wasn't terrible. She shut her own eyes. It was marvelous. The pain subsided after the initial shock and the demanding drive for release filled her with boldness. She reached for Shay's firm buttocks and drew him to her, filling herself with him. He let out a groan and thrust into her. She held him and pressed deeper. He thrust again and again, faster, harder--in a rhythm that soared out of control until she shuddered and the thunder took her. The throbbing inside her grew and exploded into a massive cataclysm that had her crying out his name over and over.

* * * *

Shay twirled one of her curls around his finger as he lay beside her, watching her sleep. He did not have an ounce of energy left to do much more than enjoy the touch of that strand of fiery silk. He had been blasted to the moon, crash-landed, and now he had to pick up the pieces of himself.

What had really happened? He must have caught her insanity. She was a virgin and he had not thought to use any protection. He closed his eyes. He had never done anything so foolish. Why didn't he listen to his *geise?*

... misfortune and even death.

With his luck, he now had a baby on the way.

He opened his eyes and gazed at Ula's sweet face. The baby would be beautiful if it took after her. Every part of Ula was exquisite. He ran his hand down the smooth skin of her arm and discovered she had climbed into the bed still clutching that odd tapestry bag.

He pushed himself up on one elbow and peered at the bag. Pressed up against her body, it appeared to be empty, but he remembered her sitting at the table and shoving a bunch of small bottles into it--along with a candle. Then there was the question of the snowshoes. Had they been in the bag last night?

Unable to contain his curiosity, he slid the bag from her slack fingers. She went on dreaming--no doubt exhausted from their lovemaking. His face reddened with a small measure of shame. It had been her first time, and he had acted like a dog going after a bitch in heat. He kissed her tender cheek and his body stirred with passion once more. Clenching his teeth together, he swore to himself.

When he opened the bag and peered inside, he did not see anything. Sliding his hand in, he found nothing--not even a piece of lint. A chill went through him. He knew he had seen her putting stuff into the bag. She carried it around as if she had a treasure inside it. She never let it out of her sight and even slept with it.

Where had she put all those little bottles? He would warn her before she left to be sure she did not leave any of her paraphernalia behind. He throat tightened when he thought of how empty his house would be without her.

It would be peaceful. Quiet, he reminded himself. *Like a tomb.*

With great care, he lifted her hand and placed the bag under it, but his fingers lingered on hers. She reminded him of the tale of Sleeping Beauty--so lovely--a princess just waiting for a kiss to wake her up.

Right. Sleeping with a princess. How crazy could he get?

Still, those full, rosy lips drew him closer with the need to taste them again--lips full of blarney and nonsense. Yes, she was a distraction, but no woman could compare to her.

He shook his head. *Careful. I don't need to be falling in love with a lunatic.* But he kept his hand on hers and drifted off to sleep with her warm body pressed close to his.

Chapter Five

"Save me!"

Meara's voice called to Ula, shocking her from sleep. She gasped and opened her eyes-- then realized where she was-- and why. Heaviness settled in her heart as she recalled the charm of the red candle. Of all the foolish things she had done in her life, that had to be the worst. Meara had always warned her, and she knew it was wrong.

Beside her, Shay appeared to have drifted off into the land of slumber. His warm breath against her ear sent a tingle through her with the promise of more passion. She gave a bitter sigh. She had wasted too much time already. It had to be noon, but she was loath to leave Shay's bed.

A surge of affection for him washed over her. She loved him--though certainly that was all due to the charm. Her emotions could not be real--and that knowledge crushed her even more for she could not imagine spending the rest of her life without him. She was promised to someone else, someone with black eyes--someone she did not know and had never met-- someone who would never make her feel the things Shay made her feel. Pain stabbed at her heart as she fingered Shay's brown hair. Sure, and he was a most handsome man. She had seen the photos of many men in her catalogs and none could compare to him.

A bitter flood of grief swept through her. She had the opportunity--right now-- while he was sleeping to take the dog. Moving with care, she slipped out of his embrace, all the while feeling that with every inch she drew away from him, she tore her own soul in two.

He would hate her--probably forever--for taking his dog, but Meara needed her. Meara had called her--perhaps with the very last of her magic. Biting her lip to keep from crying, Ula put more wood on the fire so Shay would be comfortable.

Before she left the room, she leaned over and touched his lips with hers. Closing her eyes, she savored the brief contact. If she could keep the memory forever it might help to ease the wrenching pain in her heart, but she found sorrow welling up within her so strong that she did not know if she could go on.

With a tide of anguish threatening to swamp her, she ran her tongue along Shay's lips for one last taste. Then she opened her eyes and drew away with her throat so tight she knew she could not talk.

I'll come back someday. I promise. With that thought, she turned and rushed out of the room before she could change her mind.

She stuffed the green velvet dress into Meara's bag and pulled out one of her more serviceable frocks, a brown corduroy. Donning it with speed, she threw on her socks, boots, and the cloak. Bran waited patiently for her as she lugged his food out to place it on the sled she had constructed earlier in the day.

Though drained, with muscles weary from lovemaking, she held back her tears. She wished she could remain in the bed with Shay. Without him the future lay ahead of her like the bleak landscape outside the window--frozen and cold.

When she had all in readiness, she stood in Shay's garage and dug into her pocket for the whistle Meara had given to her as a child. With the magic bag tucked carefully under her arm, she gripped Bran's fur and held onto the rope for the sled, which carried the dog's food. She put her lips to the whistle and began the simple tune Meara had taught her from the time she could walk. It was the only magic Meara allowed Ula to do, and the only magic that she could do correctly for it was the melody that carried her back to the *bothy*--no matter where she had wandered.

Today, the tune sounded more like a dirge. As she hung onto the last note, Shay burst into the garage and lunged for his dog.

"I knew you would do something like this!" he yelled as he grabbed the dog's leash.

"Saints preserve us," Ula whispered as all of them faded into the air.

* * * *

For one terrifying moment, Shay thought he had died. His body vanished into nothingness--all of his substance evaporating like rain after the sun comes out. Then in an instant, his body solidified, tumbling through the air before he crashed onto a floor and collided with Bran who reappeared in his grasp. The dog yelped as they both hit the sled filled with dog food.

Dazed and shaken, Shay clung to Bran who nuzzled him and licked him with his long, sandpapery tongue.

Then he felt the solid weight of Ula as she materialized in his lap.

"I must have played the tune too slowly," she muttered as she blinked her eyes and stared at the whistle in her hand. With a sigh, she shook her head. Her ice blue eyes glared at him. "You shouldn't have done that."

In his stupefied state, all he could think of was how hazy and soft those eyes had been in the throes of passion. That wayward idea started the heat pumping in his loins once more.

Dammit.

Rubbing his face and shaking his head in the hope of clearing it, he examined his hands, arms, and legs. After determining that all of him remained intact, he gave Ula a gentle shove to remove her from his lap. She squealed as her bottom landed with a thud on the floor beside him. With his head still reeling, he got to his feet and narrowed his eyes, unable to comprehend the scene before him. Tables and chairs lay upended in the small room. Magazines, catalogs, and books were scattered everywhere, some appeared singed while a lingering scent of sulfur hung in the air. The fire in the hearth had obviously gone out quite a while ago.

"Where am I?" *Maybe she put a powerful sedative in that oatmeal. Maybe I'm waking up from a drug-induced coma.*

"You are not supposed to be here." Ula twisted her hands in her lap. "This is a terrible situation."

"You shouldn't have tried to steal my dog--again."

"I'm only borrowing him," she insisted though her voice quivered with emotion. "Although--now that you're here, I don't know what Meara will do. Perhaps she'll have to turn you into a toad."

"Right." He closed his eyes as a headache intensified in

his skull. Why had he gotten involved with her? She needed a straitjacket along with a comfortable padded cell. Opening his eyes again, he noticed a tear slide down her cheek before she dashed it away. A pain stabbed at his heart as he saw the crushed look on her face. He had never had feelings for any other woman as he had for this one. Seeing her grief made him feel as if he had a frigid steel band around his own heart. She really got to him. Was it only because sex with her had been a mind-boggling experience?

Why was he thinking with his dick instead of his brains?

"I don't know what you did to me, and I don't want to know. I'm just going to take my dog and go home." He grabbed Bran's collar. The dog balked and refused to move.

"Bran is going to help me." Ula got to her feet. "He promised."

"Bran cannot promise you anything. He's a dog. He doesn't talk, and he belongs to me."

"He and I understand each other."

Shay glared at her. "Fine. You can talk to him on the phone."

"I don't have a phone." She lowered her head and he saw her shoulders tremble.

That's when a glacial wind roared down the chimney and Shay heard a disembodied voice calling out, "Save me!"

He went numb.

"I'm coming, Meara!" Ula stepped over the chaos littering the floor and reached for a bowl, which she placed in front of Bran's nose. He sniffed and growled. Then she grabbed a cloak from a hook on the wall and placed that by Bran's nose. He barked.

"I must go now." She hurried to the door and opened it, but before she went out, she whirled around and returned to throw her arms around Shay.

When she kissed him, his brain short-circuited. He pulled her closer, deepening the kiss, wanting to consume her, savor her, and lie with her again--anywhere--even right here, wherever it was. Bran's bark shattered the spell.

The dog had run out of the door.

Ula pushed her hands against Shay's chest in an attempt to shove him away but he covered her trembling hands with his and stayed her for a moment. He stared into her eyes, which glittered with unshed tears, and a great wave of grief hit him full force. He dropped his hands from hers.

"Goodbye." It was a bare whisper. Then she drew away, turned and ran after Bran, slamming the door behind her.

Shay's head swam. With his arms empty and another hard-on pressing against his pants, it took him a minute to get his mind back in gear. Then anger flared up and he went to race after them. When he opened the door, a cold blast of wind hit him and he realized he wore only sweat pants—no shirt, no coat, no gloves, no hat, and no boots.

Dammit.

He looked down at the floor. Clothing lay scattered here and there, along with books, and catalogs. He found two woolen socks and he put them on his feet. It was a tight fit, but better than nothing. He found a sweater that stretched out enough for him to slip into it. Then he snatched up the cloak that Ula had held to the dog's nose and draped it around himself. By the door, he found an ancient pair of old rubber rain boots. Getting his feet into the boots was no easy task. He had to curl his toes up, but he could walk--sort of.

He opened the door again. In the distance, through the pines he spotted Ula--her red hair like a beacon in the otherwise dull landscape. She trudged along after Bran with her snowshoes. Bran barked and pranced, urging her onward.

Shay called his dog, but the animal ignored him. Swearing profusely, he went after the pair, though the heavy layer of snow made his trek difficult. The frozen crystals numbed him through his inadequate clothing as he sank into thigh-high drifts, but he had no intention of allowing that woman to abscond with his dog.

Unfortunately, she had an advantage with the snowshoes. He did not gain on her at all as he clumped along, his feet cramped and half-frozen in the too-small boots. He did not have his watch with him, so he had no idea how long he struggled--although he did notice the sky darkening as evening came upon them, which added to his anxiety. If he did not catch up to Ula soon, he would certainly lose her in the dark without even a flashlight to aid him in tracking her. Bran's barks sounded faint as Shay fell further and further behind.

He realized at that point that he had no idea where he was. He had not seen a road, or even a firebreak. Where the hell was Ula going?

When nightfall descended, he finally caught up to her. She sat on a log beside a campfire, holding a pot over the flames, and stirring the contents with a spoon. The smell of food had his mouth watering.

"You should not have followed me," she told him as he stumbled up to her.

"You stole my dog." He sank down onto the log beside her, too exhausted to do anything but mumble.

"I told you I'm only borrowing him."

"He doesn't know a thing about hunting."

"He was bred to be a hunter."

"Who is Meara?"

"She's my druidess."

"Hell."

"Balor captured her."

Shay stared at her and realized that never in his entire life had he been so miserable. Desolation swept through him as he held his frozen hands closer to the fire. No one could ever be as beautiful as Ula. No woman had ever given him the explosive sexual experience that she had, but she was also completely psychotic. "How long has it been since you stopped taking your medication?"

She merely sighed and put one hand into her pocket. When she opened her palm, large, glittering scales lay against her skin. "These did not come from a fish. And surely, you smelled the stench of sulfur in my cabin."

"Rotten eggs smell the same."

"Rotten eggs don't ignite flammable materials."

He shook his head. He just wanted his dog. No, he also wanted to touch her again and hold her. To taste her--as well as some of the food she was cooking.

"There's enough for us to share," she said as if she had read his mind. "It's only beans and a bit of dried rabbit, but it should fill you up. I've made some cranberry tea, too."

Maybe he could steal another kiss from her. That would warm him up enough to make the long trek home--in whichever direction it lay. Perhaps, Bran could help him out in that regard.

"Where's my dog?"

"He's got the scent."

"Where is he?" Shay clenched his jaw together. He wanted his dog and he wanted him now.

"He'll be along." She portioned out the food into two tin plates. "He had his dog food already and decided to scout ahead. He thinks we're almost there."

His anger dissolved in an instant as he listened to the sweetness that lay in her voice, so soft and gentle with its delicate lilt. It made everything she said--even the crazy stuff--sound like a tender song.

At any rate, he reassured himself that some people did truly believe they could talk to animals, sane people--like the vet who took care of Bran.

She handed him the plate, a cup, and a spoon before she sat down next to him on the log. He could still smell the violets on her clothes and in her hair. That scent alone nearly erased every ounce of his rational thought process as images of their lovemaking flashed across his mind. His pulse raced with the memory. He fought to shove the pictures to the furthermost corner of his mind, but that seemed an impossible task with her right beside him. Heat rushed through him, all the way down to his cramped, frozen toes.

Somehow, he managed to mumble his thanks for the food, but then he made the mistake of glancing at her pale eyes--so like frost, but without the chill. He dared to stare into the very depths of that hypnotic ice--for only a moment, knowing full well the effect it might have on him. Then his world stood still as he perceived something like sorrow lingering in her gaze--something that looked a lot like farewell forever. Something

far worse than even her grief-laden goodbye. As much as he
had been trying to rid himself of the burden of this one woman,
his heart now constricted with fear. He could not lose her.

"Um ... this is good." He attempted a smile, though he
sensed it might have been a bit lopsided, but he thought he had
to say something. The deep silence in the woods suddenly felt
awkward.

"You did not taste it yet." She turned her attention to her
own plate.

"I can tell because it smells great." He scooped up some of
the food and found that her humble fare did taste wonderful,
though he knew his appreciation of it could be due to the fact
that his stomach was completely empty.

Again the hush lengthened as they ate. Shay found all the
warmth abandoning him as the tension grew between them.
His nerves wound into a tight knot.

She set her plate and cup down on the snow. "It would be
best if you stay here. I'll send your dog back to you when this
is over--after I've found Meara."

Alarm slid through Shay as he heard the door to her heart
shut and the bolts go into place. He would never see her again,
never hold her again, and never kiss her again. A wild sense of
desperation shot through him. He had not cared before, but he
did now. He would not let her go. He dropped his plate and
cup in the snow and drew her against him.

"I'll not let you dismiss me." He buried his face along the
slender column of her neck, losing himself in her glorious hair.
He slid his mouth along her fine, white skin until he reached
her lips. She opened for him and as their tongues met, a jolt
from the force of their passion slammed into him with such
power that he wanted only to sink into her cushioning folds
once more--to take her right there in the snow with the pine
boughs sighing overhead.

That's when he realized the wind had stopped. Dead calm
surrounded them while his tongue lingered on Ula's lips. He
drew back as his nerves tensed.

"Do you hear ... anything?" His whisper bounced like an
echo off the surrounding trees.

"No." She shivered in his arms. "'Tis unnatural."

Bran's yelp of pain pierced through the stillness and startled them both. Turning, they saw the dog limp into the circle of firelight. Shay raced to his pet with Ula right behind him. The dog cried piteously as he stumbled into the arms of his master.

Shay's stomach lurched with the heavy stench of sulfur and burnt hair clinging to his wretched pet.

"Saints preserve us." A fragile tremor sounded in Ula's voice. "His fur--it's been singed right off him."

Shay stared at his dog's naked flank in disbelief. The lush, gray mat of tangled hair had vanished. He moved to touch the dog's skin, but Ula drew his hand away.

"We must keep the area clean and apply an ointment to prevent infection. I have the ointment and the bandages here in the bag." She reached into the odd tapestry bag and pulled out a jar.

That's when the harsh roar echoed in the pinewoods. The sound turned Shay's blood into ice water. He lifted his gaze and froze at the sight before him. One hundred feet away, flames flickered from the mouth of a very large, reptilian creature who looked exactly like a dragon.

Chapter Six

Until now, Ula had never seen Balor, though Meara had told her many tales of the evil druid. She knew he could assume the form of a dragon and she figured he would be much like any other animal in the woods--easy for her to intimidate. However, the sheer size of this creature had her feeling more like a midnight snack.

"This has to be a hallucination," Shay muttered beside her.

"If it was, it wouldn't smell so bad." Her voice quaked along with her entire body, but it was up to her to save Meara. Mustering up her courage, she walked with deliberate steps toward Balor--even though her heart quailed as she drew closer.

"What the hell are you doing?" Shay yanked her backwards.

"I must demand that he release Meara."

"Right."

In an instant, she found herself tossed onto Shay's shoulder like a full bag of flour. He started to run with her, but she pounded his back.

"Let me go! I have to save Meara."

"I'm thinking we best save ourselves." He whistled for his dog and Bran limped after them.

"Put the princess down," Balor roared.

"Go to hell." Shay did not stop running.

"Please, put me down. I have to talk to him." Ula begged. "I must ask him to give Meara back to me."

"I doubt that he's in a conversational mood."

Balor's tail came at them from the side, slamming into Shay's legs. He fell and she tumbled into the snow.

Ula clutched her stomach as she sat up. The stench of the hideous creature sent nausea roiling through her.

Next to her, Shay took in a deep breath and shook his head. "Okay. We go to plan B. Do you have any ideas for plan B?"

Ula reached into the tapestry bag and drew out a fine

saber.

Shay took it from her. "Why can't you give me a gun?"

"I can pull anything from this bag that is in our little *bothy*. We don't have a gun."

"Dammit." He got to his feet and helped her up. "You run, and I'll distract the dragon for a while. Maybe I can lop off that tail of his."

"He's supposed to listen to me." But would he? She wrung her hands.

"I'm not about to become a hot hors d'oeuvre." Shay pulled the saber from the sheath, raised the blade high, and froze in that position. Balor had cast a spell on him.

Swallowing her panic, Ula straightened her spine and glared at the dragon.

The demonic laugher ended. "So, my dear princess, what brings you out here in the snow?"

She focused on his smoldering eyes. "Give Meara back to me."

"What? Not even a please or thank you? I'm surprised at you, Princess Ula. I do think Meara should have taught you better manners."

It wasn't working. He would not listen to her commands. Fright welled up in her. She clutched her hands into fists, fingernails digging into her palms. *Maybe he cannot see me well.* The meager glow from the campfire cast very little light. Clearing her throat, she dug into Meara's bag and pulled out the small flashlight she had gotten from Shay's friend. Turning it on, she focused it directly at her own face.

"Undo the spell on my companion," she demanded.

Balor's sigh rumbled the ground at her feet. "Yes, my princess."

Hope sprang up in her chest. She turned to look at Shay.

He blinked his eyes and glanced back at her. "What happened?"

"Balor cast a spell on you so you could not move." She kept her voice low, though she suspected the wicked creature could probably hear it anyway. "I asked him to release you."

"Fine, then. I don't want any more of his tricks."

Before Ula realized his intent, Shay threw the blade at the dragon's chest, but the razor- sharp saber bounced off the hard scales. Balor roared and blew out a stream of fire directed at Shay. The flames did not touch Ula, but she screamed with horror seeing Shay engulfed by the blaze.

The inferno withdrew. Ula's heart stopped. Shay crumbled into the snow and lay still. She stared at Shay as her knees buckled and she sank down beside him upon the soft snow. Shay had not been turned into charcoal. Not a hair on his head had been singed, though the smell of sulfur clung to him.

Balor swore. Then with a roar that shook the ground, he blew out his volatile breath and the pines surrounding Ula, Shay, and Bran burst into an inferno. This amused the fiend.

"You will not escape," he chuckled.

"Shay, my beautiful man." Ula knelt beside him, whispering as she pushed back his soft brown hair. He lay motionless, with his face as white as the snow he lay on. Frost crept over him and she felt his skin turn cold.

"You've killed him." Anger and grief shook her. "You wicked beast!"

"I will have you as my bride." Balor bellowed. "Then I will rule the Enchanted Island."

Ula did not care about the Enchanted Island or her inescapable destiny. When she kissed Shay's lips, a chill pierced through her. She cupped his face in her hands and sobbed. She loved him. She could not bear his death.

Balor had ruined everything in her life. Because of him, she had been a virtual prisoner from the time she was born. To keep her safe, Meara had kept her hidden away in the bog. She had no friends, had never enjoyed the companionship of any peers, and had lived without all the privileges that her rank should have guaranteed her.

Fury heated her blood until she became nearly breathless with the hatred burning in her chest. She got back on her feet and shot a scalding glare at the demon.

"You will never take me and you will never rule the Enchanted Island." She pointed her finger at him as she felt the

venom spilling into her blood. She loathed Balor. He had taken
Meara and Shay away from her. The two people in all the
world she loved.

Balor growled back at her. "I have the power to make you
do as I wish."

Her temper mounted as she realized that all the rules
carefully controlling her life had been useless. Setting her lips
together, she started to intone Meara's spell for turning a rabbit
into a puppy.

Balor found that laughable. "You do not know a thing
about magic."

Ula continued the incantation with her voice rising. She
included all the flaws in inflection she had used the last time
she had tried it. As she finished the last syllable, she heard a
strangled cough from Balor. A gurgling echoed above the roar
of the flames that surrounded Ula. Then in an instant, Balor
liquefied into a putrid puddle of slime.

Bran, who had been cowering beside his master, gave a
frightened yelp and sidled up next to Ula.

Ula blinked at the massive mess that had been Balor. She
lifted up the flashlight and aimed it toward the slippery goo. A
dwindling column of smoke swirled in the center, but then
skidded away as the wind picked it up and carried it off.

Numb and cold, Ula sank down once more beside Shay.
Defeating Balor would not bring back the man she loved.
Tears streamed from her eyes as she threw herself across his
chest and wept. Bran barked and began to lick some of the
frost from Shay's face. Surprisingly, she thought she heard
Shay draw in a shallow breath.

Bran barked at her and continued drawing his raspy
tongue across the face of his master. Ula pressed her fingers
against Shay's neck. Did she feel a faint pulse?

"Ula." At the sound of Meara's voice, Ula turned and saw
the druidess materialize not ten feet away from her.

"My dear child, you've freed me from Balor's
enchantment." As Meara's body solidified, she sank
unconscious into the snow.

* * * *

Ula used her whistle to get them all safely back to the *bothy*. Both Meara and Shay remained unconscious, and though Ula knew many of Meara's simple herbal remedies, nothing seemed effective. Ula was glad to have Bran's company. He kept her spirits up as best he could and did not complain about his injuries. However, her other patients had pulses so faint that Ula sometimes thought she only imagined them.

She toyed with Shay's hair and kissed his forehead, grieving as she recalled the passion and heat they had so briefly shared. It was her fault that he lay like death. Wrapped in her anguish, she berated herself for allowing him to follow her in the snow. She should have locked him in the *bothy*.

The deep pain in her heart overwhelmed her as heavy sobs racked her insides. Finally exhausted, she fell asleep on the floor beside her bed where she had placed her silent lover.

The following day, the snow began to melt. Bran dragged Ula outside and tried to get her to walk in the fresh air with him, but she had barely enough energy to sit upon a log. The sun on her face did not cheer her. Her future seemed as empty as her soul.

Bran's bark forced her to glance his way. That's when she noticed that the crocuses beside the *bothy* had bloomed. Meara had planted them long ago. The druidess loved everything about spring for it was her favorite time of the year. The thought brought on another wave of sorrow to Ula.

Smothering yet another sob, Ula fought against the weariness that left her so listless. She gathered up a fistful of the bright flowers and brought them inside. With a sad sigh, she waved the flowers beneath Meara's nose. Then she plucked one of the soft petals and smoothed it across Meara's cheek.

"Spring has come, Meara." Her voice trembled as she struggled to hold back the tears. "The sun is shining and the snow is melting."

She turned to place the flowers in a short vase and set them on the night table at Meara's bedside.

"I love spring." Meara's voice, gravelly and hoarse,

startled Ula. She whirled around and clutched at the woman's hand. But though the older woman had spoken, there seemed to be no change in her--she remained stiff and motionless with her fingers limp.

"Please wake up. I need you." Ula begged as she laid her hand upon the older woman's forehead.

Meara's eyelids fluttered but did not open. "Aye, child, but I am feeling weak. A bit of broth would do me good."

Ula thought her heart would burst. She had so much to tell Meara, but all she could do was cry. With her tears choking her, she kissed Meara's cheek.

"Forgive me, my sweet princess. I was wrong to keep the magic from you." Meara's voice faded into a quiet rustle as her hand patted Ula gently.

"I-I do not want the magic, I only want the man I-I love."

"He will come here ... someday ..." Meara whispered the words.

"I do not want a stranger. I want Shay." Ula sobbed.

"Shay? Who is Shay?"Meara's fingers tensed.

* * * *

Shay sat in the back of the boat as his father rowed the little craft out to sea. He looked behind him at the snow-covered beach, but he could not see Ula. "Where's Ula? Is she all right?"

"Remember what I told ye? Didn't I say there were dragons? I gave you two *geise* that would have saved you a lot of pain. *Thou shalt not run from the dragon. Thou shalt not pierce the dragon with a sword.* Why didn't ye listen to me words?"

"I thought dragons were nothing more than another myth." Shay watched the shore grow farther away. The smoke curling from the chimney of his house was but a wisp on the wind.

"Aye. That is your problem, me boy. You like to think you're too smart for us old ones. You are so sure that if you can't see it, it doesn't exist. You always have to have proof." The shoreline disappeared as his father rowed out into the swells.

"How many people have ever seen dragons?"

"Ah, there you go again. Believing you've got to have statistics. Facts. Pictures. You best be remembering that there are things you cannot know, and things you cannot see, but they are there just the same."

"No one will ever believe me." Except Ula, he thought.

"And what of it? Knowing the truth is all that matters."

"Aye. I thought Ula was crazy, spouting off a bunch of blarney, but everything she said was true. Do you think she's safe?" He glanced back behind him, but he could see only the rolling water about them. Even the horizon grew hazy and indistinct. Storm clouds gathered above the small boat. "Turn around, Da. We're in for a storm and I've got to see if Ula's all right."

"Ye thought ye could trick fate by saying your vows to her."

"How do you know that?" Shay stared at his father. The man looked as robust and healthy as he had most of his life, but Shay knew his father had died well over six years ago.

His father did not answer his question. "Ye cannot change destiny, me boy."

"I'm sorry about the vows. I think ... I know ... I'm really in love with her ... now."

"Ah. Is it love, me boy? Or are ye only loving her because you found out she was not lying to you?"

Shay sighed. "No. It's--there's more to it than I can say. Please, take me back. I want to make sure she isn't hurt."

"If you love her, you would swim this ocean to get back to her." His father remained silent after that, pulling on the oars with more vigor as the waves billowed higher with the strong wind.

Shay grew more agitated as he worried about Ula. Could she really handle that dragon by herself? Would the dragon let her go?

He rubbed his eyes and wondered whether she cared for him. The brief and explosive passion they shared might not mean a thing to her. What if he told her he loved her, and she turned her back on him? Could he bear the pain of her rejection?

His father pulled harder on the oars as he struggled to row against the rising storm. Shay became alarmed when he saw they were taking on water. He picked up a bucket and started to bail.

"Where are we going, Da?" He had to yell for the storm blew his words away.

"I was hoping to save ye!" his father shouted back at him.

"Save me from what?"

"From hell, me boy!"

Shay felt a chill grip him. "What have I done?"

"Ye know ye broke the *geise!*"

"Am I... dead?" Shay's voice cracked. He glanced at his arms and legs, everything looked fine.

"Just about. We've got to hurry before the devil finds out. Keep bailing."

Shay worked with all his might, but the little boat was no match for the waves. In a matter of minutes, the small craft was swamped.

"Da, we're sinking!" Shay called out as the boat dropped beneath the water.

"Then ye better swim!" His father shrugged his shoulders and then vanished.

Shay began to tread water but as he swung his gaze around he could not remember in which direction he had last seen the shoreline. With the overcast sky, it was impossible to judge whether he was headed west or east. Panic surged through him as he realized he could drown.

Struggling to stay calm and keep afloat, he tried not to waste his energy. Praying that Ula had escaped the dragon, he knew he must see her—at least once more. Even if she did not love him, he needed to tell her he loved her, with all his heart.

"Ula!" he shouted. "Where are you?"

* * * *

Ula pressed the cool cloth against Shay's forehead to bring down his fever. He thrashed about on the bed, throwing off the other cloths on his arms and chest.

She swallowed the lump in her throat. He seemed to be getting worse instead of better. Meara had warned her that his soaring temperature could cause him to go into convulsions.

Weak as she was, Meara sat beside the fire in the kitchen preparing a decoction of bayberry to lower Shay's fever, though it would only be of use if he were conscious enough to drink it.

Ula wrung out another cloth to place on Shay's arm and felt as if she had squeezed her own heart dry. She had told Meara of Shay's blue eyes and Meara insisted that if he recovered, she would have to use her sorcery on him. He must forget everything--the dragon, the *bothy*, and even Ula.

She could hardly bear the grief. Dipping her hand into the chilled water of the basin for another cloth, she remembered how Shay had carried her through the snow. She wrung out the soft flannel and placed it on his other arm, gliding her palm along his hard bicep. She loved him, but she did not know if he loved her. Perhaps, he would not be interested in marrying her anyway. After all, she had taken his dog and Bran had been severely burned.

Meara had been intrigued with the fact that Shay had not been harmed by the dragon's fire. She had checked him and not found a single blister.

"Someone must have cast a protection spell upon him," she mused. "Although, that is usually only done for certain people--dignitaries and the like--princes and so on." She had questioned Ula about Shay's family, but Ula knew nothing-- not even his last name, though it did not matter. Meara reminded her that she could not change her destiny, she must marry a man with black eyes.

Ula felt hollow inside, as if all her misery had drained her of any hope. She had told Meara of the love charm--though she had not divulged any of what happened as a result of it. However, she suspected that Meara might have guessed because the druidess gave her a piercing look and explained that what Ula had thought was a *love* charm was really a *lust* charm. She also noted that its effects were only temporary.

"Da, we're sinking!" The raspy sound that came from

Shay's throat hardly sounded like him at all.

Ula's pulse jumped and she touched his cheek. It did not feel as hot as it had an hour ago. Renewing her efforts, she wrung out another cloth and placed it on his chest. His heart thundered against her hand.

"Ula!" he shouted. "Where are you?"

"I'm here, Shay. Wake up." She smoothed back the tousled, damp hair from his forehead.

"Ula!" His voice sounded stronger.

"I'm here beside you. You're having a bad dream. Balor is dead. You're safe."

Yet, he did not seem to hear her. He flailed his arms and legs, sending the cool cloths to the floor.

Ula raced to the kitchen. "What should I do, Meara?"

"Wake him up, child," Meara stirred her brew in the kettle over the fire.

"How? He doesn't seem to hear me."

"You must divert his attention from the terror of his dream. A slap might work."

"A slap? Hit him?" Ula glanced back at Shay. She had seen him punch the bagpiper in the face. Hitting Shay could be dangerous.

She hurried back to his bedside. His thrashing had lessened, though it had not stopped. Sighing, she sat down in a low chair.

Then she bent to whisper in his ear. "I love you, Shay. I love you with all my heart."

Suddenly, Shay's restless movements stopped and his brow lifted. "Ula?"

She leaned over, intending to keep her touch brief and light, she kissed him on the lips, but he shocked her by responding. He threw his arms about her and drew her down to him. His tongue sought hers, pulling her into the sleek, wet warmth of his mouth. Passion ignited in her with enough fire to melt every bit of the snow outside. Heat stirred low in her belly and her limbs grew heavy as the craving centered between her legs in the deep, moist darkness. She knew the feeling could not be due to the lust charm since Meara had said the effects of it were only temporary. This had to be real. She prayed he felt the same way and she thought maybe he did for with his hug so fierce, she grew lightheaded from a lack of air.

"Ula," he whispered against her lips. "You're safe."

"Yes, I turned Balor into a large puddle of slime."

She felt him shudder as he drew in a great breath.

"The sword... I shouldn't have thrown it. I broke that *geise.*"

Ula frowned. "You have *geise?*"

"I broke most of them," he sighed. "How did you turn Balor into slime?"

"I used an old spell--the wrong way, but I got the result I needed."

"Am I in your *bothy* then?" His hands twined in her hair, running through the strands as if he could memorize each one.

"Yes." She stared at him. His eyes remained closed. A small knot of fear worked its way into her throat, but she reminded herself that he was alive. "Why don't you open your eyes?"

He scrunched up his face. "My eyelids are stuck together."

"I'm sure Meara has an ointment or a salve that might help." She lay her head down upon his chest and listened to the glorious sound of his powerful heart. Still the terrible memory of all that had happened tightened her voice with emotion. "I was so afraid."

"So was I." His hands massaged her back and shoulders. It seemed to ease away some of her worry. "The last thing I remember is the flames surrounding me. I thought I was going to be toast."

"Meara says someone must have put a protection spell on you."

"Must have been Da's druid when I was a kid."

"Your father had a druid?"

"Weird, isn't it? But I'm glad the protection worked."

A chill shimmered along Ula's spine. "Who was your

father?"

"Ronan Devlin."

"And his father?" Meara asked, suddenly startling Ula who had not heard her approach. Ula sat up straight in her chair and smoothed out the wrinkles in her dress.

Shay recited his genealogy. Meara listened, but said nothing--she didn't have to. Ula had spent many hours in Meara's tutelage repeating the long, boring list of names.

Shay was a prince, descended from a long line of Irish kings.

Meara applied ointment to his eyes, telling him it would take a while for the special salve to dissolve the gummy residue holding his eyelids shut.

Bran had stirred from his cozy place by the hearth, happy to hear his master's voice once more. With a rumble of contentment, the dog grinned and laid his huge head against Shay.

Ula wondered at Shay's lineage as she warmed up some broth. How strange that she had found him. She thought about it as she fed the broth to him, a spoonful at a time, until she suddenly heard the sound of a helicopter hovering low over the treetops. She sat the bowl and spoon down upon the table with a clatter as her fingers trembled.

The little *bothy* had been discovered.

Chapter Seven

"What day is it?" Shay asked as the sound of the rotor blades swooped closer. He made another futile attempt to open his eyes as a sense of alarm gripped him. The last thing he had seen was the dragon's fireball. Had his eyes been injured? Would he now be blind for the rest of his life? He was afraid to find out.

"March twentieth," Ula answered.

"Hell." He struggled to sit up. Trevor and Liam must have discovered his empty house with the truck in the driveway and reported him missing. "Didn't you call anyone to let them know where I was?"

Again the blades of the helicopter beat against the pine trees. Bran's frightened howl added to the bedlam.

"We don't have a telephone." Ula's dismay seemed evident from the quiver in her voice. "Usually Meara casts an invisibility spell so no one will find us, but she just hasn't gotten her strength back yet."

"Right." He rubbed his eyes, but he still could not open them. Even prying them apart did not work. Cold panic gnawed at him. Could he ever work again if he was blind? He felt a cold sheen of sweat beading up on his brow. "Have you got a sink?"

"I can get you a basin of warm water."

"Make it hot." He held his head in his hands as the helicopter buzzed by two more times. It came so close Shay could swear it was about to land on the roof of the *bothy*.

How in the world would he ever explain what had happened to him?

And what of it? Knowing the truth is all that matters. The words of his father came back to him. But hadn't his father spoken those words in his nightmare? Or had it been a dream? Had it been real? He scratched at the heavy growth of beard on his face and tried to sort it all out.

"Come out of the house!" An amplified voice demanded.

Bran yelped.

"We must vanish," Meara insisted.

"No. We will not leave. We will stay here." Ula decreed.

Shay was not surprised at the authority in her tone. After all, she had faced down the dragon.

"The authorities will publicize our whereabouts. You must remember that most people do not believe in the Enchanted Island." The old druidess sounded more weary than afraid. "They will think we are crazy."

"I don't want the Enchanted Island. I want Shay."

"You do?" Shay could not prevent the rush of feeling that came over him. His heart swelled and warmth spread through him.

"Yes." Ula's voice sounded closer--a gentle whisper at his ear. "Forever. I love you."

He turned to the sound of her lips and brushed her cheek. He sought the glow of her kiss and found it. Heat turned his blood into liquid fire and with it he found his strength renewed. He reached for her and pulled her against him. The swirl of emotion clutched him. He must have Ula--forever. He could not be without her.

"He is not the one. Stop this madness. You cannot throw away your destiny!"Meara pleaded.

"I repeat. Come out of the house now with your hands up."The amplified voice from the helicopter vibrated the walls.

With reluctance, Shay released Ula. "Whoever is in that helicopter means business. Could you hand me the basin with the water please?"

The touch of Ula's hands upon his as she led him to the water basin on the nightstand brought a balm to his soul. The softness of her skin belied her strength.

"Princess, we must escape," the old druidess begged.

"I am staying right here. I will run no longer,"Ula stated with calm purpose.

Bran barked as if in agreement.

"We're illegal aliens!" Meara wailed.

"You are?" Shay asked as he bathed his eyes. The gummy residue that held his eyelids together peeled away bit by bit.

"It was a matter of escaping or being killed," Ula

explained.

"Perhaps you can ask for political asylum." He would help her, doing all he could because he could not bear to be without her. And if she had to leave the country he would go with her.

"What an excellent idea. I read about that." Ula pressed a soft towel into his hands.

"Politicians do not acknowledge the power of druids," Meara droned on. "And the Enchanted Island to most people is little more than a myth."

Heavy pounding sounded on the front door of the *bothy*. Ula and Meara gasped in unison.

"I would guess that is the booted foot of a SWAT team member." Shay almost laughed. He had never pictured himself in this type of situation.

Once. Twice. The third time a crash echoed in the *bothy* as the door gave way.

"Put your hands up. We're coming in!" The gruff shout had Bran growling.

"Sit," Shay ordered. Bran gave a ferocious bark. "Ula, please tell him to behave himself."

In less than a moment, Bran quieted.

Shay succeeded in prying his eyes open. Despite the water dripping into his eyes, he could see. Relief shot through him with such force that he stumbled backward, collapsing down upon the edge of the bed while he dried his face with the towel. The towel was a pale blue and he noticed all the tiny little loops of the terry cloth. Amazing. He had never really looked at a towel until now. He had never noticed the infinite beauty of it.

He had taken so much of life for granted, but most of all he realized he had taken Ula for granted, too. Though nothing made much sense anymore, he knew that Ula was someone he could count on--delicate as she appeared, she was fearless--but she was not a lunatic. There were some things he did not understand, but that did not matter.

He took the towel away from his face and saw her as she stood with her hands in the air, worry furrowing her brow while the black garbed SWAT team aimed automatic weapons at her and Meara.

"Shay Devlin?" one of the men barked out.

"Yes, that's me."

"Your friends thought you'd been murdered."

Shay shook his head. "What imaginations those guys have." Oh if his friends only knew how far imagination could go. "You can put the guns away. These women took care of me. I had a bit of frostbite, I think." It was as good a lie as any other.

"You ladies can lower your hands. I'd like to see some ID," one officer said, lowering his gun.

Uh-oh. Shay gritted his teeth. *This is going to be a problem.*

Ula and Meara turned toward Shay. Ula gasped, but Meara passed out cold. One of the SWAT team officers caught her before she hit the floor.

"Your eyes!" Ula appeared more shaken than when she had faced the dragon.

Shay touched the area around his eyes. "What's wrong? I can see. They aren't stuck together anymore."

"They're... they've changed." Her face looked nearly as pale as Meara's. "Shay, your eyes aren't blue anymore... they're black."

* * * *

Ula clung to Shay as she brushed the wedding veil away from her face and gazed out over the water. "There it is!" She pointed off in the distance where the Enchanted Island hovered in a hazy mist at the edge of the horizon.

"That's all I get to rule? It looks tiny."

She gazed up at his smile. In a tuxedo, Shay appeared more handsome than ever.

"Actually, it's quite large--a significant piece of real estate, but it's all mine--and yours, of course," she amended. "And we won't have to stay there all the time--I know you enjoy building chimneys."

"I don't care where I live as long as it's with you, but a

secluded island would be the perfect place for a honeymoon." Shay leaned over to give her a tender kiss.

For a moment, the sizzle between them took away her breath so that she might have forgotten all about their task but for Bran whining at her side. The wolfhound had carried along a basket and he dropped it at her feet.

She drew away from Shay and bent down to pick out a trowel from the basket. Trying not to get any dirt on her wedding gown, she stuck the trowel into the grassy earth beneath her feet. "Once a year the island comes here to the coast of Antrim. We simply throw a piece of sod onto the island and it will stop floating around and remain stable."

"So *that's* why we have the cannon." He took the trowel from her hand. "Allow me."

Ula laughed while Shay proceeded to chop out several squares of sod.

"Did you get a permit for that big gun?"

"Meara taught me how to make it appear invisible if need be." Ula felt so much better knowing that Meara was getting a much-needed rest in Aruba.

He straightened up when he had several large chunks of sod in each hand and gave her a lopsided grin. "Are you sure this is going to work?"

"No." She gave him a nervous laugh. "However, after the crash course I took, I think we've got a better than average shot at this."

"If we don't succeed this year, there'll always be next year."

"Of course, but you haven't seen me in action yet with this cannon. I am hot stuff."

Shay dropped a row of kisses on her shoulder. "Sweetheart, when it comes to heat, you are in a class by yourself."

Ula felt the flame ignite within her, but she busied herself by placing the sod in the special shell casing and then preparing to fire the cannon. Despite her careful calculations, she still found her fingers trembling by the time she finally lit the fuse. All her life, she had been waiting for this moment to take on her rightful role--to stop cowering in fear in the bog, but having Shay beside her was even far more precious. As the shell soared out over the water, she turned to him and leaned against him, closing her eyes.

"I'm afraid to watch."

The sound of his beating heart calmed her. Then she heard the distant explosion.

"Bull's eye." His voice rumbled in her ear.

She turned around to see that the sun had broken through the clouds and sent streams of glorious rays upon the island. The faint, indistinct spot on the horizon bloomed before her eyes, the pale colors strengthened into vibrant life.

"You did it." He pulled her close and gave her a lingering kiss, full of needy hunger.

"I guess it's time to row out to our kingdom." She had to force herself to break the contact.

"Good thing I can row fast." He scooped her up and hurried to the boat with Bran lopping along behind them. "Do you know what I'm going to do when we get there?"

Ula nodded her head and ran her tongue along her lower lip. "Tell me--slowly--and in great detail."

The End

Penelope Marzec grew up along the Jersey shore. She started reading romances at a young age and fell hopelessly in love with happy endings. Now a retired teacher, she spends her days writing uplifting stories.

You can find her website at:

http://www.penelopemarzec.com

Read her blog:

http://penelopemarzec.blogspot.com

Like her Facebook page:

http://www.Facebook.com/penelopemarzecbooks

Or follow her on Twitter:

@penelopemarzec

34041624R00049

Made in the USA
Middletown, DE
21 January 2019